Ernie Gonzales

Escape from Paradise

Written by Beth Shepherd
Illustrated by Anait Semirdzhyan

instant
ap◻stle

For my precious niece Chloe, keep shining brightly!

Also to Dennis and Lynn, thank you for all

your love and support and for sharing

beautiful Comares with me.

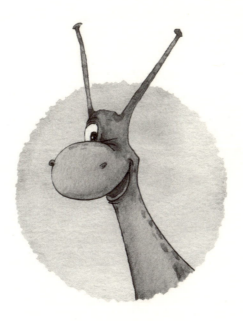

The shadow

A group of snails sat huddled together at the edge of
Olive Garden. They had been up all night keeping guard
after Bruce had posted them there. Now they were
convinced it was all a joke. Eighteen hours on watch and
nothing, not even a single leaf falling or the sound of trees
rustling. Sleepy and fed up, they gathered their things,
put out the campfire and tied up their rucksacks. Irritated,
they brushed off the bits of spinach that they had spread
over their shells as camouflage and took off their cherry-
pip army hats. In silence they started to slide down the
hill to report back to their leader.

Suddenly, a shadow appeared over their heads.

It was dawn. The sun had just broken through the trees
and the garden was already buzzing with life. As the
morning sun pulled the garden into the day, the small
group watched as the mysterious shadow passed over
their heads in the direction of the village, plunging it back
into darkness as black as the night sky. It had caught
them off guard, and all they could do was watch,
powerless to stop it as it crept sinisterly along the garden
floor. Bravely, one of them grabbed a small rolled-up leaf
which was sticking out of the backpack carried by the
snail in front of him. Trembling, he blew through it with
everything he could. The eerie sound echoed across the
village, shattering the peaceful quietness of the early
morning and alerting its residents to the suspected
danger that was descending upon them.

The whole community of snails stopped and looked up, wondering what had interrupted their usually peaceful morning. Some came outside to see what was going on. Many froze in terror, watching through windows as the shadow engulfed their houses and filled them with darkness once again. Those who were still fast asleep were rudely woken, and sat bolt upright in their beds, shocked by the haunting sound that had penetrated their dreams, only to find themselves surrounded by darkness on what would normally have been a bright, sunny summer morning in their beloved snail garden nestled by the river in this picturesque Spanish village of Viñuela.

The shadow had now found its way even to the very edges of the garden, covering everything in a thick black blanket of darkness. Squinting, the snails tried to make out the shape of the shadow that was looming above them. As suddenly as he had started, the snail stopped blowing on the leaf.

For a moment there was nothing but silence. Then, out of nowhere, there came a terrifying scream which caused hearts to stop beating for a split second. All eyes turned to where it was coming from: near the back of the garden a young snail was sliding towards them as fast as he could, yelling from the top of his lungs, tentacles waving in all directions. Every snail began to panic as their eyes searched to see what he was fleeing from. When they spotted the large pair of black boots towering behind him, their hearts fell to their stomachs. Some fainted at the sight before them; others fled. Only the brave ones allowed their eyes to follow the boots upwards on what seemed to be a never-ending journey towards the sky until eventually the figure above their heads became hauntingly clear.

Towering above them stood a very large man. He was holding a big net in one hand and a brown cardboard box in the other, and he was staring straight at them.

The great snatch

Ernie and his grandpa, Manuel, had risen early to go for their usual morning stroll, which consisted of a lap around the garden and a meander along the river. Then they would make a slightly more energetic climb up to the top of a large mound on the edge of the garden, which overlooked the small village they had so carefully created.

The pair were very fond of one another and savoured every moment of their time together. Ernie had always admired his grandpa and had grown up wanting to be just like him. Manuel was wise but adventurous, young at heart and free-spirited. He knew that his grandson was a lot like him and he enjoyed teaching him all he could about life, and the things Ernie had achieved so far in his young life made him just about the proudest grandfather anywhere to be found.

The two always looked forward to their morning walks, but recently Manuel had been growing a little tired of his grandson's constant complaining about his best friend, Bruce. On one of their recent outings Ernie had grumbled for the whole duration of their walk. Manuel resisted the urge to say something and instead faithfully listened. He suspected that Ernie just needed someone who would listen to him.

Bruce and Ernie had been good friends for a while and were almost inseparable, but they were very different characters. Manuel had come to understand that differences needn't be a bad thing if you learn how to use those differences well. But the two friends hadn't quite grasped that concept yet. Secretly, Manuel wished Ernie would hurry up and get it, so the two could go back to chatting about everyday stuff like the weather.

On this ordinary morning they were sitting on their favourite log that overlooked the garden, enjoying another glorious sunrise over their little piece of paradise. Manuel, who had an eye on his paper and an ear on his grandson, was the first to spot the dark shadow out of the corner of his eye. He slid his glasses back on his nose, looked up and squinted as he tried to work out what was going on.

Ernie, who had finally finished another long speech, awaited his grandpa's response. But all was quiet. 'I bet you haven't heard a thing I've said, have you, Papa?' he said as he turned to see if his grandpa was paying attention.

'Are you seeing what I'm seeing?' said his grandpa. Ernie heard panic beginning to rise in Manuel's voice and turned to see what his papa was looking at. Ernie was just about to answer when Manuel grabbed him and pulled him under a large leaf to hide.

Bruce had just returned from an early morning jog and was on his way to meet the young snails to relieve them of their lookout duty, when he was suddenly engulfed by the darkness. He stopped in his tracks. Suspecting his worst fears had come true he nervously looked up to the sky. 'I guess I was right,' he whispered to himself, as he let out a long, sad sigh.

Most of the snails of Viñuela were just starting their day. The garden was bustling with life as hundreds of snails were busying themselves with daily tasks, when their peaceful village was suddenly covered by the strange, dark shadow. Some froze in silence as they tried to figure out what was going on, but most began frantically yelling at the top of their lungs. It was mayhem. They all began sliding in different directions to try to escape, but no one seemed to know where to go.

'Looks like we're gonna be snail meat, cobbers,' said Bruce under his breath, as his heart fell to his stomach in despair.

At that moment, the huge net came crashing down into the garden and scooped up every last snail. Bruce's words rang in his own ears and he was thrown forcefully, along with the others, into the dark and dusty cardboard box.

Ernie and Manuel watched from under their leaf, where they were out of danger. 'Papa, please tell me this is not what I think it is,' Ernie said quietly.

Manuel remained silent, unable to speak as his brain tried desperately to work out what was going on. Ernie watched in horror as the big man closed the lid of the box, lifted it onto his shoulder and marched out of the garden.

Ernie and Manuel gasped. 'P... P... Papa, are you reading what I'm reading?' said Ernie, struggling to get the words out. Helplessly they watched as their whole family, along with everyone they knew and loved, were stolen from them before their very eyes. The man carelessly threw the box into the back of a van and slammed the door. Then he got into the driver's seat and sped off up the hill.

Ernie felt his stomach turn and his head spin as he watched in shock. Barely able to focus, he just about managed to read the words 'Restaurant Carmen' that were painted on the side of the van before it completely disappeared out of sight.

The night watchman

Bruce was a strong and fearless Australian snail. Usually nothing fazed him, but this rattled him to his core. In the chaos, he had hit his head against the inside of his shell and had instantly passed out. The last thing he remembered before the net had scooped him up was seeing Ernie and Manuel peeping out from under a leaf on the mound just on the edge of the village. Now they were all he could think about. He hoped they had managed to avoid the same fate as everyone else, as he suspected they would be the snails' only hope of rescue.

Finally his head stopped spinning and he popped it out of his shell but he couldn't see a thing – not even the end of his nose. It was pitch black. Suddenly he became aware of a heavy weight bearing down upon him. Terrified and confused, his heart pounded loudly in his shell as panic rose, but slowly his eyes began to adjust to the dark. He held his breath, afraid of what images might emerge before him.

Soon he managed to make out the rim of his own shell and his limp tentacles hanging down over his face, and he let out a sigh of relief. But his relief was short-lived. As his eyes continued to work out the shapes around him, he soon discovered that one of his worst nightmares had come true: he was buried under a pile of snails.

They were everywhere; he was tightly closed in on all sides. It was like a horrid snail prison. No matter how hard he looked, he could not see daylight anywhere. Bruce hated confined spaces, except for his own shell, and he had always had a fear of being trapped.

He wondered just how many snails were on top of him, pressing down on his fragile, thin shell. He let out a loud yell in terror.

The hundreds of other snails, also dazed from the impact, began to come round. Immediately, they too cried out in shock. Soon, all that could be heard was a chorus of snails yelling. The noise in the box was deafening.

As the panic escalated, the snails began squirming to free themselves, but this just caused them to pack themselves in more tightly around each other, putting them in further danger.

Bruce took a deep breath and shouted as loudly as he could: 'Enough!' His heart was pounding louder and louder by the second. Immediately, every snail popped inside its shell. There was momentary relief as everyone became silent and sought comfort in the familiarity of their mobile home. Bruce breathed in the silence as he tried to make sense of what had just happened. 'I knew it,' he said to himself.

Over the last few weeks Bruce had been making secrets visits back to the compost heap where he had first met Ernie, his friend and fellow snail, so long ago, and where their whole adventure had started. The compost heap was close to the road, and from there Bruce could see everything that was going on in the village and make sure that nothing uninvited or unwelcome was going to attempt to enter their precious Olive Garden. However, what he had observed during his recent nightly visits had really unsettled him. Three large and greasy-looking men had begun to meet regularly in the park to chat about something that seemed to have made them all very angry. Bruce listened diligently to their conversations, sensing a growing frustration among them.

It didn't take Bruce long to figure out that the men had all recently lost their jobs and that they were concocting a plan of some kind. Then, two nights ago, everything had become devastatingly clear to him. He had discovered that they were actually a group of unemployed chefs who had been fired because they could no longer meet the demands of their customers since snails had disappeared off the menu and the restaurant had closed.

Chefs usually go snail hunting when it's raining, as the rain always draws the snails out; like bugs to a light, they just can't resist. There had always been a constant supply of them in the village of Viñuela, but a few months ago it seemed that they had completely disappeared. The chefs had even set up spray hoses through the village and the park to draw them out, but they had caught nothing – not a single snail. Now the men were on a mission to put snails back on the menu and get their jobs back. They seemed desperate, and Bruce knew they would be prepared to do anything to find those snails.

Bruce knew exactly what had happened to the snails of Viñuela, why they had disappeared a few months ago and where they had gone. He and Ernie had been the ones behind their sudden disappearance. Before the pair had first met, Ernie had discovered a huge pile of empty snail shells behind a fridge in a human's house. His discovery had prompted him to go on an epic mission to rescue every single snail from the village and to bring them back to live in the Olive Garden with him, a place which, along with Bruce, Ernie had risked everything to find. The news of the empty shells had spread rapidly to every other snail in the surrounding villages and they had all gone into hiding.

Bruce had suspected for a long time that the local people ate snails, but he had really hoped it wasn't true. He knew it wouldn't be long before the chefs would discover the Olive Garden and the snails' secret hideout.

He had finally gathered all the information he needed to tell Ernie but he was reluctant to say anything as he wasn't sure how Ernie would respond. It had taken him two days to pluck up the courage, and he was planning to tell him that very night. He had really been hoping his friend would believe him.

He let out a long, sad sigh as his thoughts came back to the current situation he was in. He realised now that he had left it too late to tell Ernie and to warn everyone. Frantically, he tried to think of something to say to the others that would make it OK, but he couldn't think of anything that would be helpful. So he stayed quietly curled up in his shell and covered his ears to protect him from the sobbing and yelling that was coming from the hundreds of snails around him. Normally he would have been quite smug to realise that he had been right, but now all he could do was wish that he had been wrong.

Buried dreams

In the darkness of his shell, Bruce tried to block out the noise of the other snails, which was matched by the sound of his heart pounding. It echoed inside his shell, and was so loud he could hardly think. He popped his head out for a second. There seemed to be calm now among the other snails, but he wondered how long for. He knew he wouldn't survive buried under a mound of snails – none of them would. He had to do something. He had to be brave, but he didn't really feel like it; Ernie was the brave one, the one with all the ideas. Beginning to panic again, Bruce popped back into his shell and tried to think good thoughts to calm himself down.

His thoughts drifted to his good friend Ernie. He smiled as he thought of him. Ernie was such a dreamer, but not just a daydreamer: he was a determined dreamer and an inspiration to Bruce.

The two had first met when Ernie had suddenly landed on Bruce's prized compost heap on the edge of the village. Bruce thought Ernie had flown through the sky, until he found out that he had been thrown from a compost bin out of someone's kitchen window above the compost heap. Despite his disappointment when he discovered that Ernie wasn't really a flying snail, Bruce was secretly impressed by his great escape from the kitchen where he had been held captive as a pet. The two quickly became friends and spent a lovely evening sharing stories of their adventures. Bruce would never forget how he had felt when he first heard Ernie's story: he had set off on a journey to find the legendary Olive Garden, a mythical snail paradise at the bottom of the village that he had spent his life dreaming about.

It had been his amazing grandpa, Manuel, who had filled Ernie's head with wonderful dreams about the place, through the stories he had been telling him since he was a small snail. However, no one in their village believed the Olive Garden existed, except Ernie and his grandpa. Manuel was an adventurer just like Ernie, and when he was young he had gone in search of it, but had never found it.

Inspired by his papa's stories, and tired of living in a dusty plant pot by the side of the road, Ernie decided he would follow in his grandfather's footsteps. He knew without a doubt that he would find the garden. Confidently, he left his home and set off, leaving his family behind. Little did he know that he would end up trapped in a kitchen as someone's pet. So when he finally escaped and met Bruce on the compost heap, Ernie was about as determined as a snail could be to prove that the garden existed.

Bruce had been fascinated by Ernie's determination to pursue his dream at all costs and was quite happy to help him on his way, although he didn't really believe in the garden. Eager to have his compost heap all to himself again, Bruce had decided to help Ernie. However, what Bruce hadn't realised was that he would soon become swept up in the adventure and that Ernie's dream would become his dream too. Before long, the pair found themselves riding wild dogs, cruising on the back of rubbish trucks and surfing on turtles. Bruce loved adventure, but he could never have imagined that they would not only manage to find the garden for themselves, but that they would also successfully rescue all the snails of Viñuela. It warmed his heart that the snails were now able to live safely together in the Olive Garden and the snail village they had created within it.

Bruce had really admired Ernie's ability to dream such big dreams, and he knew he could never dream like that. He just wasn't a dreamer like Ernie – or at least he didn't think so. If someone needed a job done, he was the snail to do it. Give him a plan or an idea and he would put it into action straight away. Together they made a great team.

Bruce felt his racing, anxious heart begin to calm down as he reflected on the fun of their adventure and all that they had achieved together.

They had been living in the Olive Garden for a while now. The snails had carefully built the whole village together, and life was good there. It was better than good: it was more than he could ever have imagined. Each snail family had their own home to live in, built out of mud and leaves; they had snail schools and universities, restaurants and cafes. But the best place in Olive Garden was Lemon Harbour, a place where the two friends enjoyed watching the sun set across the glorious lake situated in the middle of the garden. Bruce and Ernie spent many an evening sailing out from the harbour on a leaf boat across to the restaurant on the other side. Olive

Garden was everything Ernie had described it would be, and so much more.

Ernie had been convinced that his paradise dreamland was all they needed, and that they would all live out their days there forever without any trouble. However, Bruce, being a tough snail from the Australian outback, had had a life full of ups and downs and had learnt that it wasn't always that simple. Trouble sometimes creeps up when you're least expecting it, which is why he knew better than to ever let his guard down and become complacent. He had tried on many occasions to explain this to his friend, but Ernie just didn't want to hear it: he refused to allow his illusion of a perfect paradise garden to be broken. Despite that, Bruce couldn't ignore his instincts, which had been telling him for a while that this paradise garden may be too good to be true. So he diligently kept one eye open for trouble while making the most of his new life for as long as it lasted.

Adventure was in his blood. Deep down he craved it, but now he wished he hadn't been so right. He hadn't had the heart to tell his beloved friend that he had been sneaking back to his old home. Now he really wished he hadn't been so hesitant. Instead, he wished he had been brave enough to stand up and take the lead. If he had managed to convince his friend, maybe right now they would be making a plan together instead of feeling all alone.

The invasion of the thug slugs

Cautiously, Ernie and Manuel emerged from under the leaf and looked around them. There before their eyes lay their beloved garden, usually so full of life and joy, but now hauntingly empty. Right in the middle of it were two large footprints, as if to remind them exactly why it was so empty. Ernie shuddered and wondered if anyone had been squashed under them. Never had he been so upset in all his life.

They scanned the garden with their eyes; there was not a single snail in sight, alive or squashed. Hoping to find that some had been left behind, perhaps hiding under their beds, they both dived into their shells and rolled themselves down the hill and into the main part of the garden.

'Hello!' shouted Ernie.

'It's OK, you can come out now,' added Manuel, but no one answered. In desperation they explored each snail home, but not a single snail could be found. It seemed that every snail in the garden, apart from them, had been captured.

Gloomily, they checked the very last house. Finding nothing, they closed the door behind them and turned with their heads hung down to the floor and walked down the path, wondering what in the world they would do now.

'Well, well, well, what do we have 'ere, then?'

Ernie and Manuel, lost in thought, jumped in fright at the sound of the gruff voice. They looked up to discover that they were face to face with a group of menacingly fierce and angry slugs.

The snails froze. Second to being squashed on the pavement, slugs were their most feared threat and were despised by snails everywhere. For as long as snails could remember, slugs had targeted them and bullied them. Being peaceful creatures, the snails rarely retaliated, and instead did everything they could to avoid the slugs and their hateful attacks.

Ernie suspected that they were jealous because snails had something that they could never have: shells. He doubted the slugs would ever admit that, though. In spite of their size, which was almost double that of a snail, slugs always felt inferior to them, and for that reason they had become bullies and spent years terrorising the snails, invading and stealing whatever they had. They were thugs, and now they had somehow found their way into the garden.

Trying to not seem afraid, and conscious of the urgency of their situation, Manuel slid up to the large slug. 'I don't care what you want or how many of you there are. You need to get out of this garden now!' He was too old to be afraid of a bunch of slugs.

The slug peered down at Manuel. 'We want your garden,' he said, as he spat all over Manuel's small, wrinkly head, 'and we will not leave until we get it.'

Ernie pulled his grandpa back. He had been afraid that would be what they wanted, and he wondered how long they had been watching and waiting for their opportunity to seize it. They had obviously seen the other snails being captured. However, the pair didn't even have time to think about the details of their situation as the slugs slid forward and seized them. Ernie and Manuel tried to slide away, but there were too many of them. The slugs lifted them up and carried them out into the middle of the garden. Then they hoisted them high above their heads and flung them forcefully against a nearby tree, pushing their shells into the sticky sap that was oozing out of the bark.

Frantically, Ernie and Manuel tried to wriggle free, but they were well and truly stuck. Helplessly they hung there and watched as the slugs laughed and made fun of them. Finally, after they stopped laughing, and when they remembered what it was they had come to do, they turned their attention to their plan to destroy the garden. Ernie and Manuel were powerless to stop them and could only watch as they set out to crush everything the snails had carefully created.

Time to reflect

The slugs were huge and strong and it took them only seconds to destroy what had taken the snails weeks to build. Maliciously, they slid from house to house and threw their large, slimy bodies down onto each roof, crushing it under them like they were crushing a matchbox. The slugs laughed as the small mud houses crumbled under their weight.

'Leave it alone, you thugs!' yelled Ernie as he watched a group of large slugs pulling down the garden's favourite cafe, the place where Ernie had so many fond memories of hanging out with his family and with Bruce.

Ernie began to boil inside with anger as memories of how his family and friends had lovingly created this magical place flashed through his mind. Now he was watching it vanish before his eyes. His papa turned to him, 'Ernie, it's alright. Let them have it; our family is more important.'

Ernie paused and took a deep breath. He turned his face away from the slugs and closed his eyes. 'You're right, Papa.'

Both hung on the tree in a silence that was filled with sadness. Ernie felt tears welling up in his eyes. Eventually he spoke: 'I should have listened to Bruce,' he said, finding it hard to get the words out. Manuel turned to look at his grandson. 'He was trying to warn me about this, Papa.' Ernie hung his head in despair, tears rolling down his face. 'If only I had listened to his warnings.'

It had been just over a year since they had arrived in this paradise garden. It had very quickly become their home, and the snails had been thriving in the small, secluded piece of land hidden among the lemon trees on the edge of the village of Viñuela. The amazing adventure Bruce and Ernie had been through together to find it had really brought them close as friends. But recently their friendship had been under strain. Over time, Ernie had become irritated with Bruce's constant whining about a supposed threat that he believed was about to descend upon the garden, and that they weren't safe any more. It was driving Ernie crazy and ruining his peaceful life. He could have handled it if it had just been between the two of them, but then his friend seemed to be preparing for an imminent attack by creating a snail army: he had already begun sending some of the younger snails on a nightly watch.

Ernie had been annoyed that his friend had seemed intent on unsettling everyone in the garden with his imaginary threats. Ernie had worked so hard and risked everything to bring the whole snail community of Viñuela to this place, and he had not been prepared to ruin it over silly fear tactics. Plus, this was *his* dream. He had held on to it for so long, knowing that one day he would find paradise. Now he had reached it, he had refused to believe that what they found was anything less than a promised dream come true. So he had chosen to ignore Bruce's warnings.

At first they had argued; then they had both decided to not speak to each other, and that was where they had settled. In recent days they had hardly seen each other: Ernie had remained on one side of the garden in his own little world of paradise, and Bruce had stayed on the other, rounding up the younger snails who seemed to enjoy the drama of it all. Division had crept into their peaceful haven.

Ernie had tried to keep the community calm and told them not to listen to Bruce's babblings, but he had sensed that panic was quietly growing and felt powerless to stop it. The only one who seemed to share in his frustration was his grandpa Manuel, although even he seemed to be fed up with it all.

But now Ernie's heart felt as if it had dropped out of his chest and was rattling around in his shell as it dawned on him that he was wrong to have ignored Bruce's warning. This was his best friend, the one who had helped him navigate so many obstacles and challenges to reach his precious dreams. Without him he would have ended up back in his old family home, the dusty plant pot by the side of the road, living off vegetable peelings along with the rest of the village. He realised that he had truly let his friend down.

Sensing Ernie's thoughts, Manuel snapped him out of it. 'Now is not the time for blaming yourself. That's not going to do anyone any good,' he said firmly. 'We need to focus on what we can do to rescue them.'

Ernie turned to look at his grandpa. 'Papa, they're gone. Don't you get it?! They've been snail-napped and are probably well on their way to a local kitchen by now, to be thrown into a pot of boiling water.' As he said the words his stomach churned over and he felt nauseous.

Manuel looked at his grandson. He knew he was right and he knew it didn't look good for the others. But as Ernie's grandpa he knew that his job was to offer words of wisdom and encouragement. After all, if there was any chance of the snails being rescued, Ernie would be the one to do it. But only if he snapped out of this defeated, gloomy mood and found some inner courage. A few home truths were in order to shake him up a bit. Manuel turned and looked at him. 'Ernie, you are my grandson. I have always believed in you and have been behind you in all that you do. Your belief in your dreams has inspired us all, and it's because of you that we have enjoyed a new home in Paradise. But recently you've had your head in the clouds and you haven't been aware of the reality around you. It's good to dream, but we must also keep our eyes open to what's going on around us. Otherwise trouble can just creep up and hit us right between the eyes.'

Ernie turned his back on his papa. He didn't want to hear any more.

'And now you have to open your eyes and see what is around you, and dream once again.'

Ernie wasn't ready to admit it, but his grandpa's words created a bubble of determination deep in his belly.

'Maybe life has a new journey for you to take. You must be brave and follow it. Who knows, maybe there are more exciting adventures to be had, more opportunities to be found and others to help.'

Ernie turned and looked into his papa's warm, brown eyes.

'This life isn't just about you and your dreams; it's about others too. Right now, Ernie, your friends need you, and we can't give up without a fight.'

The words cut deep and were hard to hear, but they were words that really made him think.

Ernie knew that everything Manuel was saying was true. He felt a lump in his throat and swallowed hard to get rid of it. He realised he had become complacent. With sadness, he thought of his friend Bruce. He wished he was here right now and Ernie would tell him that he was sorry for not listening to him.

The bubble of determination grew stronger in his belly until it was ready to burst. 'THAT'S IT! Papa, you're right. We have to find a way! They need us and we can't abandon them! I'm ready for a new adventure!'

Both snails were fired up and ready for the fight that lay ahead of them; however, they were still stuck hard in the sap of the tree. Unable to move, they hung there, trying to think of a way out of their sticky situation.

It was Ernie who broke the silence. 'I have a plan!' he whispered. Eagerly he told Manuel his great idea.

'Amazing, Ernie!' replied Manuel, once he had heard enough to be convinced. 'Let's do it now. There's no time to waste!'

Both snails took a deep breath and called out to attract the attention of the thug slugs.

The bargaining tool

Slugs love destroying things, especially things that snails have created. So stomping over everything they had built in their stupid garden was the most fun the thug slugs had had in ages. As they trashed the place they couldn't help smiling to themselves; finally they had come up with a plan against the snails that had actually worked. For hours they had been waiting on the edge of the garden, ready to take it over. If they couldn't have their very own shells, they could at least have snail paradise and make it their own.

Over the last few weeks they had been watching diligently from the road as the chefs created their plan. They knew everything, including when they were going to snatch the snails from the garden. So that very morning, before dawn, they had left their home in the sewerage tunnel by the road for the last time and headed to the Olive Garden. They had laughed to themselves as they surrounded it, hiding under leaves and waiting for their time to invade. They watched the snails awaken to a beautiful morning, knowing their precious home was about to be destroyed forever.

With delight they had watched as the head chef from Restaurant Carmen walked right into the garden and, with one swoop, scooped up every last snail. Well, except for those two, thought one of the large slugs as he looked up at Ernie and Manuel, but he wasn't bothered about two small, lousy snails stuck to a tree. He had his garden, and now it was time for a bit of redecorating.

'Hey, slugs!' yelled Ernie. Instantly, all the slugs stopped what they were doing and looked up. 'I think you should know that this garden gets really cold in the winter and blazing hot in the summer,' Ernie said. 'You'll never survive without a shell to protect you.'

All the slugs gasped.

'Get on with your work, you lazy thugs,' shouted the large slug to the others. He seemed to tower over all the others and they appeared to be afraid of him. Ernie figured he was the leader, as he'd noticed that the others called him 'Boss'.

The large slug turned and slid menacingly towards Ernie and Manuel. 'And what's it to you?' he said, spitting green slime in their faces as he talked.

Manuel took over: 'Look, I'm an old snail and I've had more than enough drama in my life. Take the garden. It's not worth the fight for it. But we're just warning you that without a shell it may not be the paradise you think it is, that's all,' he said, trying to sound confident.

'That's right,' added Ernie.

The slug paused for a minute, trying to think. Ernie could see his brain struggling to work. He knew that slugs' brains were virtually non-existent, but even so he thought it best to not let him think for too long. 'Looks like you've led all these slugs here for nothing,' Ernie chuckled sarcastically. 'Now it's spring, and as soon as summer comes you'll all be nothing more than black shrivelled pancakes stuck to the leafy floor. Not even good enough for bird meat.'

The large slug drew right up to Ernie's face. He hated snails: they were always so smug, with their perfect lives and their perfect mobile homes. 'Is that so?' he said.

Ernie winced as the smell of the slug's rotten breath filled his nose, and he tried not to look into the black depths of his foul mouth. Ernie noticed something moving inside the slug's head, and as he looked closer he could see a small brain inside it, whirling at great speed. It looked as if it was overworked and might explode at any second.

'Nice try,' said the slug, suspecting he had thought too much and was beginning to overheat. 'But you won't get rid of us that easily.' He breathed his foul breath over them once again, then turned to walk away.

'That's OK,' replied Manuel calmly. 'As I said, I've had enough of fighting. Just let us go free and we'll tell you where you can find your very own shells to live in.'

The slug stopped in his tracks and turned back to look at Manuel. All the other slugs, who had been trying to listen, heard the words 'your very own shells' and looked up. Ernie and Manuel had got their attention; they knew that slugs were desperate to have their own shells. If the snails were clever, the slugs could be about to play right into their hands.

Ernie went on, 'But we'll only tell you if you set us free first.'

The slugs had been presented with a decision. They didn't like decisions: it meant they had to think, and this was a tough one. They tried to remain cool and continue to look threatening, even though their heads felt as though they were about to rocket launch off their necks. They suspected it was a trick but they couldn't work out how, and having their very own shells was just too tempting for them. So eventually they agreed. 'Let them down!' shouted the Boss. On his command, the slugs rushed over and pulled Ernie and Manuel down from the tree.

Now the snails were down on the ground again they felt very small as they looked up at the thug slugs towering over them threateningly. 'You'd better not be playing games with us or we'll crush you inside your precious fragile shells,' shouted the Boss fiercely, as green, slimy drool dripped down from his mouth and onto the snails. Ernie and Manuel's hearts were pounding with fear, but they had to hide it and remain calm: there was too much at stake.

'Well, if you don't want to believe us then we won't tell you, and you'll never enjoy the benefits of finally having your very own mobile home, safe from birds,' said Ernie as he smugly rubbed the side of his shiny beautiful shell.

'OK, OK! Just get on with it,' replied the Boss, trying to keep control of the situation. 'Take us to these shells, then, and do it quick – it's getting hot already.'

'OK, my slimy friend,' said Manuel, trying to humour the brain-dead, green lumps of slime. 'Be patient. First we need to get our things, and then you'll need to follow us back to the compost heap.'

This took a bit of convincing but eventually the slugs agreed. They followed the snails back to their house, not allowing them out of their sight for a second.

Box of memories

Ernie and Manuel quickly slid into their house, leaving the slugs waiting anxiously outside, peering through the window. Thankfully it was one of the few houses the slugs hadn't yet crushed. Ernie slid to his bedroom and retrieved a box from under his bed. Inside was a sketch pad full of drawings and plans from his last adventure, as well as some random, useless items that he had packed before he set off to find this garden so long ago. These items had in fact proved to be far from useless. He smiled at the joy of seeing everything again; it all brought back a flood of good memories from his last adventure.

But there was no time for reminiscing; with every second that went by their friends were in more danger. Reaching up to the cupboard above his bed with his tentacles, he pulled down his trusty old rucksack. Then with haste he filled it with as much stuff as he could; after all, he may never return to this place again, and everything he owned would be gone forever. Then he packed important supplies such as cabbage leaves, avocado and water.

'What do you think will happen, Papa?' said Ernie as he rejoined his grandpa.

'I really have no idea, son, but at least we've bought ourselves some time to think,' replied Manuel.

'Yeah, and who knows – maybe we can find a way to escape when they're not looking,' said Ernie.

'Maybe, Ern. I'm confident that we'll find a way out of this situation and get on our way to rescuing the others. But I think we need to face the fact that we've lost our garden,' added Manuel sadly.

Ernie flung his old rucksack onto his shell and tied up the straps. Somehow it brought a feeling of strength, and he felt a wave of courage take over him. Then he nodded to Manuel and the pair slid out through the door.

Knowing that these could be their last moments in the Olive Garden, they slid gloomily to the river's edge. They could sense that the slugs were growing anxious as they approached the water, and Ernie wondered how in the world they had managed to get through the rapids in the river to reach the garden. He suspected that they didn't know the snails' secret to travelling on the river, and he wasn't about to reveal it to them. It was clear that they would have to endure a rougher ride than they were used to. Bravely, they encouraged the slugs to board the leaf boats. Then the Boss dragged them into a boat with him so he could keep a close eye on them.

The slugs knew their way to the compost heap and led the way along the river. The snails had to paddle as fast as they could just to keep up, while the Boss lay back to enjoy the ride. Soon Ernie's thoughts wandered back to the place where the empty shells were. It was a place he had promised himself he would never think of again. He had discovered them while he was being held captive in a kitchen as someone's pet. Ernie shuddered as he thought about it. Life as a pet had caused him to grow lazy and he had almost let go of his dreams, so he began to do laps around the top of the fridge to keep active and stay determined. But one day he fell behind it, and to his shock, he landed on a massive pile of shells. The discovery had confirmed to Ernie that humans did eat snails, but at the time he didn't want to believe it.

At that moment, their leaf hit the raging rapids and he snapped out of his thoughts. The boat began to tip from side to side, and water began to spill in. The slugs began to squelch and slide in the mixture of slime and water. Desperately they tried to take control and steer their boats but they just slid from side to side shouting, 'We're going to die!' 'I don't want to die without a shell!' 'Argh!' Ernie and Manuel were small, and as the boat filled with water they felt their heads disappearing under the surface.

Just as they thought they might well drown, Ernie and Manuel heard a voice from the water: 'Ern, are you OK?' They felt their boat being lifted slightly out of the water, just enough for the snails to catch their breath and poke their heads over the side of the boat and see a pair of big eyes staring at them.

'José, is that you?' whispered Ernie as he recognised his old friend. Manuel coughed and spluttered beside him. 'What are you doing here?' asked Ernie, as he turned to see what the Boss was doing. Thankfully he was still half submerged in the boat and trying to pull himself up by his tentacles.

'Don't you want a ride, mi amigo?' answered the large old turtle as he popped up out of the water next to him.

Ernie was so excited to see his friend that he nearly fell off the leaf. 'Oh José, am I glad to see you?!' he exclaimed. 'Don't let the slugs know you're here,' he added quietly. José quickly slid back into the water, out of sight of the slugs.

'José, the snails have been taken – all of them!' Ernie said, too emotional to make sense.

'What do you mean, Ern? Surely those slugs aren't strong enough?' José replied, looking confused.

'No, it was a large human,' replied Ernie. 'He came in and stole everyone, and we're the only ones left.' José was speechless. 'And now these lousy slugs have taken us as prisoners.' José gasped as he listened to Ernie's story. 'We're trapped. I don't know if we'll be able to escape to try to rescue the others.'

The turtle looked over at the large slug who had now managed to pull himself upright again. 'It's a sad day for the snails,' he said, feeling concerned for his small friends. He had known the snails for a long time and enjoyed helping them whenever he had the chance; he had carried them through these very rapids on his back many times. 'Leave it with me,' he said with a wink, then quickly slipped under the water and out of sight.

The large slug looked at Ernie suspiciously. 'What are you doing over there?' he shouted, as a wave of water knocked him to the floor once again.

'Nothing!' replied Ernie innocently.

'You'd better not be planning anything or I'll come over and pluck you out of your shell right away,' gurgled the slug as he splashed around in the water at the bottom of the leaf boat. Ernie shuddered.

Finally they were through the rapids. Exhausted, they stopped paddling and drifted for a short while. Ernie looked back at the garden as it vanished out of sight. He couldn't believe he had handed it over so easily to brain-dead thugs, and now it was gone forever. His heart fell into his stomach. But he knew that it was the right thing to do, and that the lives of his friends and family were far more valuable than a piece of land which was empty without others to share it with.

So he bravely turned his back on the garden and looked towards the compost heap. 'You'll find the shells behind the fridge in the kitchen up there through that window,' he said as he pointed to a small window high up on a wall above the compost heap.

The slugs all looked up at the window. It was so high. For once, they were speechless.

A frozen end

The rusty old blue van screeched to a halt outside Restaurant Carmen in a small village in the mountains. A large, sweaty, bald chef stepped out of it and walked into the restaurant carrying a big, brown cardboard box and stomped up the stairs to the kitchen. Inside the box hundreds of frightened snails bounced up and down as they feared for their lives. Bruce hid inside his shell, feeling nauseous. He remembered the story Ernie had told him when they first met, of how he was carried in a veggie box and was nearly squashed between two beetroots. Never in a million days did he think he, too, would end up in a box, fearing for his life.

'Help us, Bruce!' panicky voices all round him called out. 'We can't see!'

Bruce knew those at the very bottom of the box were in considerable danger, but he didn't have a clue what to do. So he just slid deeper into his shell, hoping this was all a dream and he would soon wake to find he was safe in the Olive Garden. 'Why are they asking me?' he mumbled as he slid deeper into his house. 'Ernie's the one who's good with ideas.' He covered his ears and hoped they would look to someone else to be their hero.

Then suddenly, out of nowhere, an idea popped into Bruce's head. He knew it was an idea that Ernie would be proud of. There was no time to waste; with every minute that went by, those at the bottom of the box were in increasing danger of losing their lives.

Bravely, Bruce popped his boggly eyes out of his shell and shouted, 'Listen up! I have a plan!' Those who could, shot their heads out of their shells before he could finish his sentence, desperate to hear about his plan. 'Right, first I need you all to stay calm. If you panic and scramble this won't work, and it could kill those at the bottom.'

Everyone gasped. Bruce knew it was harsh to say, but he also knew he couldn't risk a dangerous rush. 'Those of you on the very top and who are near the side of the box,

I want you, one at a time, to stick to the edge and begin to slide yourselves right to the top.'

Luckily, the box was only about three-quarters full, despite every snail in Viñuela being inside it, so there was some room for everyone to carefully manoeuvre. The snails didn't hesitate, and those near the edges began to climb, shaking in terror as the box wobbled with every step the man took. As soon as they were well on their way, Bruce called out to those closer to the middle to slide out towards the edges and to follow the others to the top. Then he asked everyone else to begin to fill the gaps and to make their way to the edges. The snails responded quickly and worked well together. Soon there were masses of snails sliding up the sides of the box.

'Fill in the gaps! I don't want to see any gaps between you,' Bruce yelled. 'You must be shell to shell,' he shouted to those who had already made their way up to the top. It was an amazing sight, and Bruce was reminded of the day when he had organised these very same snails to take their exciting trip on the back of the turtles, along the river from the compost heap to the Olive Garden. He had surprised himself by the way he had been able to take the lead when he needed to. Now was no different. Maybe his friend was right – perhaps there was more to him than he had once thought. However, there was no time to think about how he felt right now: the snails needed him. Confidently he continued to orchestrate his clever plan.

Bruce scanned the area and was happy to see that every snail was out of danger and stuck to the side of the box, with the remaining few lining the floor. Now that he could see into the bottom of the box he called out to make

sure they were all OK. All popped their heads out –
except two. The whole box of snails fell silent as Bruce
quickly slid across everyone and down to the bottom of
the box. As he drew nearer he heard sobbing; they had
lost two snails in the crush. It was two of the older ones;
they were weak and had been easily crushed. His heart
sank.

The footsteps were now stomping along a hard
concrete floor, a door slammed and then it felt as though
the man was climbing up some stairs. The snails wobbled
precariously and used all the strength they could find to
stick to the box. As long as every snail managed to remain
stuck to the side, no one would be in danger of being
crushed. Bruce could feel a sense of relief from the group,
despite their sad loss. There would be time to mourn for
their friends soon; now everyone was looking to him for
what they should do next.

'Shh!' he shouted. Quietness fell immediately. Bruce
listened as he tried to work out what was going on
outside. Suddenly the footsteps stopped, and what the
snails heard next made their slimy bodies begin to
tremble and wobble like jelly on a plate.

'Here are the snails you asked for,' came a loud voice.
'It's a good catch. They're all plump and juicy.'

'Great!' came another voice. 'The mayor will be
pleased with this.'

The snails gasped and began to panic once again. They
had no idea what they had been taken for, but they were
sure it wasn't good. Desperately, they all began sliding in
different directions. Order began to turn to chaos. Some
lost their grip and fell to the bottom of the box again.

'STOP!' yelled Bruce. 'We still have time. It's not over yet. We must stay calm so we can think of something.'

But it was no use. The hysteria grew and grew as the snails began to talk more and more loudly.

'BE QUIET!' he yelled assertively. 'We need to know where they're taking us!' But he couldn't be heard over the noise of hundreds of panicking snails.

Bruce felt very alone and wished Ernie was with him. The noise in the box was so loud that they didn't even hear the fridge door open and slam shut. The noise only began to subside when they felt the temperature drop. Bruce instantly realised where they were, and knew that with every second that passed they were drawing closer to a chilly end.

A slimy escape

Ernie and Manuel slid off the leaf boat and onto the bank of the compost heap. By now it was midday and the sun was getting hotter by the second.

'Right, you weeds, you're going first up that wall,' shouted the Boss. 'If it's a trick you're playing on us then at least we'll know.'

With force, his thug friends shoved them forward onto the mound of rotten vegetables. Desperately, Ernie looked for José, but he was nowhere to be seen. The group began sliding towards the wall. The nearer they got, the taller it appeared to be.

For a second Ernie felt a flicker of joy as he remembered the amazing feeling of being thrown out of the vegetable scrap box through the window and feeling the fresh air on his skin for the first time in ages. Winning his freedom back had felt exhilarating, and now he couldn't believe he had lost it again. As if that wasn't bad enough, he now had to go into that awful kitchen once again and relive a horrible memory he had tried so hard to forget. He began to doubt his plan and wondered if they should have just stayed stuck to the tree instead. Manuel, almost as if he were able to read Ernie's mind, nudged him and said, 'Chin up, son. It's not over yet; we'll still have time to think of something.' But the closer they got to the wall, the more elusive the idea of escaping seemed to become, and even Manuel began to accept that they would have to make the long journey up to the window, which at his age might well be the last thing he were ever to do.

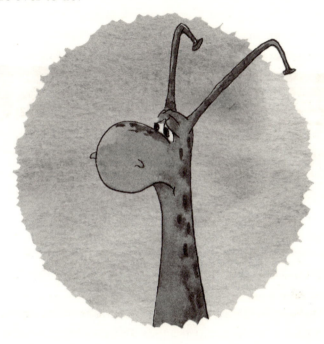

As they trudged forward, deep in thought, a loud roar thundered behind them. Snails and slugs froze. The slugs began to tremble as they nervously turned to see what was behind them. Ernie and Manuel tried hard to hide their beaming smiles; they knew exactly what had made that frightening roar.

As the group turned around, there, towering above them, was a terrifying black monster with green seaweed hanging over its eyes and drool dripping from its sharp, snarling teeth that looked ready to chomp them up. The slugs yelled and tried to move back, out of its way. Ernie and Manuel stayed where they were and pretended to be frozen on the spot with terror. The monster roared again. The force blew their tentacles back and almost pulled them off the floor. The slugs were shaken to their core. Then the monster swooped down and scooped up Ernie and Manuel in its arms, teeth gnashing and gurgling noises coming from the depths of its mouth.

'Aargh!' yelled Ernie, trying to sound convincing. 'I'm so scared!'

'We're going to die! Run for your lives!' shouted Manuel in the direction of the slugs.

The slugs didn't need to be told twice. They turned and slid as fast as they could towards the wall.

'Up to the window, slugs. You'll be safe in there,' added Ernie.

When the slugs were finally out of earshot, the three burst out laughing. José whipped the sea grass off his face to reveal his kind, hazel eyes.

'Very convincing, my friend,' said Manuel, his belly aching from laughing. 'José, you make a very scary river monster.'

They looked over to the slugs. Many had made it to the wall and were fighting over who would go up it first.

'Stupid slugs!' said Ernie, but Manuel and José could see Ernie was still shaking.

'Don't worry, my son. Those thugs found out what we snails are made of,' Manuel said reassuringly.

Ernie felt himself relaxing. 'Come on, let's get on our way before they realise they've been tricked.'

After checking that the slugs were not looking, José put Ernie and Manuel gently down on the soft compost heap and quietly slipped back into the river, 'Shout if you need me,' he said just before his head disappeared under the water.

The snails turned away from the river and looked up towards the village. From where they stood they could see the park, the road that led into the village and some of the houses. They had seen the village many times from the compost heap, but today things seemed to be different. It was the middle of summer, people were out and about, and there was a buzz of activity. From what Ernie could remember it was not normally this busy.

'Papa, we need to get up on to the road. Maybe from there we can work out how to get to that restaurant,' said Ernie.

'Yes, that's what I was thinking,' replied Manuel as he watched the people walking around in the town. 'But with so many people out and about we're very likely to get squashed flat. Then we'll be of no use to anyone.'

'You're right,' said Ernie. There was a long pause as the snails tried to think of what to do next.

'The cats!!' Ernie shouted suddenly, breaking the silence.

'What?!' said Manuel who was deep in thought.

'We need to ask the cat family to help us. If we can sit on their backs, then the people won't bother us.'

Manuel smiled at his grandson and nodded. He knew that his grandson had greatness in him, and he enjoyed watching it begin to emerge once again.

Immediately, the snails began calling at the top of their voices, 'Estella, it's us, your old friends Ernie and Manuel. We're on the compost heap!' But it was no use; their voices were lost among the sounds from the bustling village.

'Here, let's use this!' cried Ernie, as he began to slide over to an empty milk carton.

Manuel knew exactly what he was thinking, and he knew it was a brilliant idea. 'Great thinking!' he said as he watched Ernie slide inside and call to the cats. His voice boomed out across the compost heap as it was amplified through the carton.

Ernie couldn't wait to see his old friends again. He smiled to himself as he thought back to how they had met. Even in his wildest dreams he could never have imagined becoming friends with a group of cats. He had first met them when they were starving and living under a bin, desperate for anything that resembled food – including snails. However, he and Bruce had managed to convince them to help them find the Olive Garden, and in exchange they promised to show them where they could find a never-ending supply of food: the compost heap. Ernie had hoped to come and visit them more often, but life had just become so busy in the garden that he hadn't had a chance. He hoped they were still there.

Eventually Manuel spotted three cats peering down from a balcony on the side of a house by the road. 'I think it's them, Ern, look!'

Ernie poked his head out of the carton and strained to see. But they were far away and he couldn't be sure. Then the three cats disappeared from the balcony. There was an anxious pause and Ernie wondered what was happening. Then suddenly, three cats dashed out of the front door of the building and across the road, bounded across the compost heap at great speed and skidded to a halt right in front of the snails.

Ernie and Manuel held their breath inside their shells as they watched and wondered if they were about to become the cats' breakfast. But to their relief, the cats began purring excitedly.

'Estella, it *is* you!' shouted Manuel relieved. The cats, Estella, Porscha and Rose, were very excited: it had been such a long time since they had seen Ernie and his friends, and they couldn't wait to find out what had been happening.

The three cats towered high above the two tiny snails. The kittens, Porscha and Rose, were now almost as big as their mum, Estella. They looked fat and pampered. Ernie wondered what they were doing in a human's house. He decided he would save the catching up for after they had rescued the rest of the snails.

The two cats looked down fondly at their small friends. It didn't take them long to realise that there was something wrong with the snails. By the look on their faces it was obvious they had not come back to the compost heap for a holiday. With haste, Ernie and Manuel told them what had happened. The three cats were horrified. Ernie then asked them what was going on in the village and Estella explained that there was a large festival taking place that day. She went on to tell them that she had heard news of an even bigger festival soon to be held in another village – one that was offering free giant paella to celebrate its reopening.

Ernie gasped as a thought popped into his head. He tried desperately to ignore it but he couldn't escape it. The more he thought about it the more he realised that all the pieces pointed to one thing, and he didn't like it one little bit…

Three soggy cats

The snails sat and looked up towards the village. It definitely seemed to be busier than usual, and they could feel the loud music vibrating across their shells. 'Come on, Ernie, let's find out where they've taken your friends. Jump on our backs!' urged Estella.

'Maybe we should wait until tomorrow,' said Ernie, feeling unnerved by his recent conclusion.

'That's not like you, Ern,' said his papa sharply. 'The fiesta might help us work out where they've taken the others. We haven't got time to waste.'

Ernie knew he was right. So he slid up onto Rose's back as quickly as his snail body would carry him. Manuel needed a bit of a helping hand from Estella. He wasn't as fast as he used to be, and she carefully picked him up with her mouth and put him on Porscha's back. Once the snails were nestled in the soft fur of the kittens, the cats took off at full speed. They bounded across the compost heap, leapt over the wall, and turned on to the road. Then suddenly Estella skidded to a halt as she found herself in the middle of a large crowd of people going in different directions.

'Shoo!' shouted a large lady in a brightly coloured flamenco dress. Ernie looked down at her shoes, bright red and shiny with long pointed heels. 'Whoa, those things would flatten me in seconds,' he mumbled. 'Keep moving, Rose!' he encouraged.

'I'm trying,' she said, as other people began shooing her out the way. Another tried to kick her, and one man nearly trod on her tail. Panicking, she looked around for her mother, but she was nowhere to be seen. 'We have to find cover,' Rose shouted to her sister.

Estella found herself being pushed towards the park by the crowds and was feeling totally disorientated. It was crazy – there were people everywhere, moving in all directions, and she couldn't see anything other than legs.

Suddenly, Manuel spotted what they were looking for. 'There, in the tunnel!' he cried, as he remembered the place they had hidden the previous time they were in the village.

The two young cats tried their best to reach the tunnel. Desperately, they wound their way around legs and balloons and bikes and pushchairs, even dogs on leads, but it was no good: the sea of obstacles was never ending.

Just then, in the middle of the chaos, Ernie spotted a large poster. In big, bright letters it said, 'Summer Fiesta', and under the words was a picture of a large dish of steaming paella. Reluctantly he allowed his eyes to read what was written under the picture, and there in big, bold letters were the words: 'SNAIL PAELLA'.

'Aargh, I was right!' he yelled. Panicking, he almost slipped off Rose's back.

'What is it, Ern?' said Manuel, clinging anxiously to Porscha's fur as she skidded to avoid a wheelbarrow full of watermelons.

'It's true! LOOK!' Ernie's tentacle pointed to the poster, shaking with fear.

Manuel looked to where he was pointing. 'Oh dear, that's not good!' he said as he peered through his spectacles. 'Where is it?'

Ernie turned again and looked at the poster, hoping to see where the fiesta was going to be held, but at that moment loud music started blaring through a speaker nearby, and huge blobs of white fluff began to fall from the sky.

'It's a foam party!' yelled Porscha.

'A what?!' asked Ernie, who was now hanging by just a tuft of fur on Rose's neck and feeling very unsettled.

'Wow, awesome!' shouted Porscha.

'No, this is not good,' said Rose sternly, hoping her mum would soon find her way back to them.

'It's a what?!' shouted Manuel. But before anyone could answer, the two young cats and their small passengers were swept up in a wave of foam that came whooshing down the hill like a small tsunami.

Ernie strained to see the poster as it whizzed past his eyes. 'Comares! The fiesta is in Comares, Papa!' he shouted. 'Where in the world is that?'

'I have no idea!' Manuel yelled back as they whooshed around a corner. The two cats tried desperately to stay together, but they were soon separated as they were spun around in the foam, like soft toys in a washing machine.

Eventually the foam spat them out and the soggy cats surfaced on the edge of the village, away from the fiesta. 'Comares is th, th, that way…' spluttered Rose, pointing to the road out of the village. 'And it's really high up in the mountains,' she added, hoping that Ernie wasn't going to suggest they go there.

'Are you still there, Ernie?' asked Manuel.

A faint groaning came from deep within Rose's fur. Ernie coughed and spluttered as he cleared the foam from his lungs and wiped it out of his eyes. 'What in the world just happened?' he asked, dazed.

'Wow, that was amazing!' replied Manuel, who had lost his glasses in the commotion.

Ernie looked at his grandpa and shot him a puzzled, slightly disgusted look. He wondered if he was getting younger or older.

'Party celebrations, Ernie. Towns love fiestas. Any excuse for a party and everyone goes mad,' said Porscha, who seemed to have gracefully surfed through the foam.

'Yeah, they have one or two every year. Most cats – most sensible cats – stay well away until it's over,' said Rose, looking pointedly at her sister, knowing full well she took any chance she could to sneak out on fiesta nights to join the party.

Ernie suddenly realised one of the group was missing. 'We've lost Estella,' he said.

'I know,' replied Rose, feeling a little tearful. She was very close to her mum and was worried something had happened to her.

'Rose, she'll be fine. She's our supermum, remember,' reassured her sister.

Ernie smiled as he remembered what a strong cat Estella was, and deep down he knew she would be OK.

Ernie and Manuel slid down from the cats' backs and the group looked around them to see where they were. The foam had taken them to the edge of the village. Behind them was the road leading back to the village and the party, and in front of them was a bigger, busier main road. The group stepped back quickly as a car came racing around the corner, music blaring loudly, narrowly missing the cats. They knew they had to keep moving but they had no idea which way.

'Did I hear someone say the village is high up?' asked Ernie, as he tried to straighten up his tentacles which were still stuck across his face.

'Yeah, it's awesome, hey!' shouted Porscha. Manuel looked equally enthusiastic, even without his glasses.

'Over there!' yelled Rose. 'There's a signpost.'

They all squinted to see what it said.

'I can't quite make it out,' said Manuel, struggling to see anything.

While Manuel stood there squinting, Ernie, who had finally got himself together, found an empty coke bottle and slipped inside it.

'It says com, com, com… um, p, comp, comp,' mumbled Manuel. 'Oh, I don't know. I wish I could read it.'

'Will this do instead?' shouted Ernie.

Manuel turned around to see two enormous eyes staring at him. Shocked, he jumped back in his shell.

'It's me, Papa. Do you like my binoculars?'

Once Manuel realised it was Ernie, he began laughing hysterically from inside his shell.

'Do you know how funny you look, Ernie?' Manuel slid and joined him inside the bottle, and then the cats turned them around so they could see the sign. While they were figuring it all out, the kittens dashed over to check out the bus stop.

'Comares. It's Comares, Papa, the same village that's having the snail paella. Come on, let's go,' urged Ernie.

The cats, who had been able to get a good look at the bus stop, called back to the snails. 'It looks like we need to go into the big city first, before we can get to Comares,' said Rose.

Ernie felt his stomach do a double somersault.

'Awesome!' cried Manuel.

Ernie looked at his grandpa. His fearlessness was incredible. He really missed Bruce right now: he would have understood his nerves.

A bus to nowhere

Two cats and two snails sat at a bus stop by the road on what was another scorching summer's day. Hiding in the corner of the bus shelter, and desperate to stay out of the sun, the group huddled together in a tiny patch of shade. Eagerly they awaited the arrival of the bus, dreaming of enjoying the cool air conditioning inside. They sat there confidently, as if they had done this a thousand times.

Suddenly Rose broke the silence. 'Wait a minute!' she said. 'What are we thinking?'

The others turned and looked at her.

'Cats can't go on buses,' she continued. 'We'll never get away with it.'

Ernie agreed, shocked that none of them, including himself, had thought about it sooner. He was sure the heat of the day was beginning to take over their brains and causing them to go into meltdown. They had been so busy contemplating the enormity of taking a bus to Comares, via the big town of Vélez Málaga, that they had failed to consider how, and if, they could even get on the bus.

'You're right, of course, Rose,' replied Ernie, feeling a little silly for getting so lost in the excitement of the plan without considering whether it could actually work. 'Looks like you two will have to stay here.' He looked at Rose and Porscha sadly. They looked so disappointed, but they knew he was right. The cats were sure to be seen and would be shooed off the bus.

This made the whole thing a hundred times more challenging. Ernie and his grandpa would have to go it alone, but how in the world would they get on and off two buses before the doors closed without the cats to carry them? It would be virtually impossible for them to slide onto a bus quickly enough. Everyone sat there in baffled silence. The only thing Ernie could think of suggesting was that they could try to wedge themselves in the grooves of the tyre of the bus. It wasn't the best plan he had ever had, and he wondered just how dizzy they would be after spinning around and around for what could be hours. But it was all he could come up with. Just then he heard the loud roaring sound of the bus approaching in the distance. Ernie felt his heart drop to his stomach; he knew there was no going back.

Ernie looked at his grandpa, who still hadn't found his glasses and seemed to be talking to a snail-sized leaf. He was just about to open his mouth to quickly tell him his not-so-great plan when suddenly they were plucked off the floor as the kittens grabbed a snail each and lifted them onto their back. 'We've got this one!' shouted Rose. Manuel had no idea what was going on.

The bus screeched as it came to a halt in front of them and made a loud hissing as it released its brakes. The cats waited from the corner of the bus shelter for the doors to open, their hearts pounding loudly. They had no idea how long they might have before the doors closed, and they didn't want to miss their chance. They were definitely the only ones planning to get on the bus, so they knew they may only have seconds.

The driver pressed the door release and they were flung open as if they were about to fall off their hinges.

The cats didn't hesitate. Instantly they leapt through people's legs as they stepped down to the floor. They bounded up the steps and dived under the seats. In less than a minute the doors had closed again and the bus driver was pulling away.

One lady was standing outside waving her arms, shouting, 'CAT!'

The bus driver thought she was just waving goodbye. 'Crazy lady!' he mumbled as he waved back, pretending to be interested.

Estella, who had been looking everywhere for her girls, bounded up the road to the bus stop, just in time to see them leaping up the steps and the door closing behind them. Her heart sank as the bus pulled away and out of the village, taking her two precious daughters with it. She had no idea if she would ever see them again, and she hadn't even had a chance to say goodbye. She let out a sad miaow.

Slugs of doom

Back on the compost heap, the thug slugs had successfully made their way to the wall and were now scaling their way up the side of it. Ahead of them lay an open window which led into a kitchen. The slugs were suspicious of Ernie and Manuel's plan, but right now, getting inside that kitchen and finding those shells seemed a whole lot more appealing than being eaten by a river monster. 'That's assuming there even are any shells,' the Boss wondered, but decided to keep his doubts to himself.

'Move yourselves, bozos!' shouted the large Boss slug who was up front with his two sidekicks beside him, leading the expedition up the wall.

The rest of his brain-dead cronies followed behind. 'What's wrong with you, you lazy thugs?' he shouted in annoyance, as many of them were lagging behind. They were a strong bunch and, because of their size, were able to do much more than snails could do, but they were also lazy and didn't like exerting much energy.

'We're going as fast as we can, Boss!' said a large one with a tuft of hair on his head.

'You're a slave driver!' said another. The Boss rolled his eyes as his lazy companions complained constantly as they dragged their slimy, overweight bodies up the vertical wall, which was now almost unbearably hot from the midday sun.

'It's so hot, Boss, we're going to fry!' they yelled.

But the Boss was determined to get those shells, and he was not going to stop for anything. 'Get on with it, you lightweights,' he replied angrily, 'or it will be me who'll be frying you in a cooking pan!'

At long last, the front line hauled themselves over the window ledge, but what they saw before them made them stop dead in their tracks. It appeared that another bunch of slugs, rather ugly looking and fierce, were already inside the kitchen. They stood face to face with nothing but a panel of glass to separate them. No one moved, and their brains whirled like a rusty washing machine as they tried to think what to do next.

Seconds later, the slugs who were following closely behind hauled their slimy bodies over the window ledge and bumped straight into them. Turning to them, the Boss shouted, 'Get back!'

'What, Boss?' they asked, as they continued to press forward up the wall and over the ledge.

The Boss turned back to face the threat before him and realised that the group inside had now doubled in number, and was continuing to grow rapidly before his

eyes. A strange-looking mob of slugs had beaten him to it
and were probably on their way to collect those shells.
'Those snails! They'll pay for this!' he yelled in anger, as
he made a fist with his tentacle and threatened the
gathering army that stood before him. He noticed that the
chief slug seemed to mimic his every action. 'You think
you're so smug? Well, wait until I get in that kitchen – I'll
show you a smug slug!' he yelled threateningly.

'What is it, Boss?' said one of his sidekicks.

'We've been sold out,' the Boss replied. 'These slugs
have beaten us to it. Those lousy snails played us for
fools.'

'Oh yeah, that's right, whatever you say, Boss,' replied
the short, fat one, completely confused by what the Boss
was talking about. 'Don't worry, Boss! Those snails are
probably sliding their way down into that river thing's
stomach right now.'

The comment only infuriated the Boss even more.
'Yeah, and that means they're not even alive for me to
take revenge on.'

As they stood there, arguing among themselves and
trying to decide what to do next, the trail of slugs behind
them continued to make their way up towards the
window. Slug after slimy slug hurled itself up onto the
window ledge, adding to the numbers. Soon there were
so many that it looked like a giant slimy pile of green
mess, as all the slugs stumbled over one another.

'I said stop! Don't you listen to anything I say?'
mumbled the Boss, as his face was squashed up against
the window in front of him.

'What's going on, Boss?' they yelled.

'Window! We've hit a window,' the Boss yelled in reply, noticing that the slugs inside were copying everything they did. 'They're making fun of us,' he growled. 'You wait until we get in that kitchen – you're done for!' He was being pushed closer against the glass as the slugs continued to arrive on the ledge. 'Will someone tell those slugs to STOP!' he said, trying to shout.

'What did he say?' asked a slug from further down the wall.

'I think he said keep going,' replied another.

'I can't wait to get my shell,' said the first as he eagerly slid up towards the ledge.

'Yeah, me too. I want to be first so I can pick out the best.'

'No, I want first dibs!' shouted another.

'Yeah, right, mate. Not a chance,' replied the first.

'STOP!' yelled the slugs closest to the window, who were rapidly becoming buried under the other slugs.

'Ooh, what funny squidgy things do we have here?!' buzzed a small voice above their heads. 'A crazy pile of slugs! First I find crazy snails chasing crazy dreams, now I seeing crazy slugs climbing crazy walls.' The voice continued, 'What's wrong with you slimy green things? You never stay still in one place.'

'Get lost, vermin!' yelled the Boss. Slugs hated flies nearly as much as they hated snails; they always seemed to be around, ready to steal their food and wind them up.

'Ooh, no! Captain Pablo not going anywhere. This too much fun to watch – you slugs so stupid,' said the fly, as he prepared to enjoy watching the slugs struggle. By now the pile was growing so big that the weight of all the slugs was beginning to pull them back down over the window ledge.

'Adios, amigos!' said the fly laughing to himself as he watched them rolling back over the ledge.

'You will pay, fly!' yelled the Boss angrily.

The slimy green ball began gathering speed, collecting those who were still on their way up as it went.

'OK! OK, you disgusting fly! Help us,' yelled the Boss. 'Tell us how we can defeat those slugs so we can get in the kitchen.'

'Ooh! Yes, maybe I will. But first, you call me "Royal graciousness", and second, you tell me what you do for me,' he buzzed smugly. 'Hey, what you want in this kitchen anyway?' He chuckled as he watched, and the slugs grew more panicky. 'OK, you not tell me, I not help you. Have nice journey, my green squidgy amigos.'

Captain Pablo's head spun round and round as his eyes followed the ball of slugs sliding down the wall. 'Ooh, you make me so dizzy, my head spinning. Too dizzy. I am off!' he buzzed as he began to fly away.

Managing to catch his breath, the Boss shouted, 'OK, there are shells in there. Loads of them, and we want them so we can live in the Olive Garden.'

The fly stopped dead in mid-air, 'Mmm! I like it!' he said, smiling cunningly to himself. He had been wanting to live in the Olive Garden since he had first met Ernie ages ago, but the snails wouldn't let him in and had banned him from ever entering it. He couldn't believe it. He was so annoyed with those lousy snails. He had helped Ernie find that place, and even interviewed him for the *Bug News*. He had thought he could go and live in the garden and run his own newspaper called *Buzzed Off!* But Ernie would have none of it.

'Hmm, this very interesting,' he said, dancing confidently around in the sky.

'Pleeeeeeeease, Captain Pablo!' called the voices under the pile that was now at least halfway down the wall and heading for a sticky end.

Warm green mush

In the fridge, the snails were growing colder by the second. Hundreds of tiny teeth chattered as they shivered inside the big white metal box. Bruce looked around him and could see that the snails were beginning to turn a little blue, himself included.

'What will we do Bruce?' came hundreds of desperate voices. 'Bruce, do something!' 'Help us, Bruce, please!'

The calls came at him from all sides, and he felt completely closed in. It was just too cold to think straight, and the pressure was too much to bear. He didn't have a clue how to help himself, let alone everyone else. Just because he had had one great idea, now it seemed they had all decided to put their life in his hands, and he felt himself going a little crazy. Panic was beginning to bubble up inside him like a pot that was about to boil over. He could take no more. Rudely, he slid across everyone and rushed to the top of the box. Then he pushed as hard as he could against the roof. To his surprise, the box wasn't sealed down and he managed to lift one of the flaps enough to be able to slide out.

It was even colder outside the box. Bruce remembered how Ernie had told him that he had felt his tentacles begin to stiffen on his head when he had found himself inside a fridge. Bruce began to realise that he had fallen into the same fate and that they were all doomed. He had failed them.

Quietly he sat there in the cold. Now he understood how Ernie had felt when he took on the great responsibility of helping others. Bruce could feel the responsibility bearing down on his shoulders. 'I'm not Ernie,' he said to himself, but deep down hoping the others would hear him. 'I don't do these things. I'm a loner and I take care of me – that's all I'm good for,' he whispered as he slid deep inside his shell. 'I'm not heroic like him.' His words only made him feel worse about himself.

Bruce sat and listened to the silence. Suddenly, in the stillness of his thoughts, a memory flashed across his mind. It was when he and Ernie had sat on the compost heap and Bruce had listened to his friend tell him about the moment he had nearly given up on his dreams. Ernie had fallen, splat, inside an avocado and had thought that it was all over, but the avocado had actually warmed him up!

It was as though a light bulb had gone off in Bruce's head. He was so desperately cold that he would do anything, even dive into a rotten avocado, if it meant he could warm up. He looked around and saw a large box of the green, mushy fruit. It took great energy to move as he was stiff with cold. Finally he slid deep down inside and allowed its warmth to melt his icy snail body.

Selfishly, he indulged in the green mush, with no intention of ever emerging. He allowed himself to forget the plight of the hundreds of others freezing to death in the box next to him.

A few minutes passed and Bruce was now warm and toasty. Feeling a little more relaxed, he let his eyes scan his surroundings. It wasn't as dark inside the fridge as Ernie had described, and he wondered why that was. Looking around him he saw a beam of light streaming across a large watermelon. Following the light with his eyes he realised that it was coming from a corner at the top of the fridge. Instantly he felt a glimmer of hope, so he popped out of the avocado and slid up towards the light as fast as he could. When he got there he found a small hole. He pushed himself through it with ease and within seconds he was sitting on top of the fridge. Looking around, he quickly discovered he was inside a dingy kitchen, all in darkness apart from the moonlight streaming in through the window.

There was an eerie silence, and he didn't like it one bit. Hanging from the walls were huge, sharp chefs' knives and large cooking pots, and he wondered if the chefs used them for boiling snails. 'Aargh!' he yelled. 'Gotta get outta here!' He spotted a door on the other side of the kitchen and began to slide across the top of the fridge towards it. But strangely, he just couldn't move. It was as if he were frozen to the spot. 'Come on, Bruce, ya potato head, what's wrong with you?' he said to himself. Trying again, he pushed forward. 'I can't help them,' he mumbled, knowing his conscience had got the better of him. 'It's just not possible,' he said, trying to convince himself. He knew he would never be able to face returning to the Olive Garden, but at least he could go back to the compost heap.

He tried to think of a big enough excuse to carry on towards the door, but there was nothing big enough. His head dropped as shame descended upon him. 'How can I leave them all there?' he asked himself; then he paused and let out a long sigh. In that moment he knew that not knowing how to save the others did not give him a good enough reason to walk away from them. 'Snap out of it, Bruce, you're better than this!' he rebuked himself, shocked at his own behaviour.

Suddenly he knew that he could either be a big snail and try, or be a small snail and regret this for the rest of his life. 'I may not be a hero like Ernie, but I can't leave them,' he said bravely. 'Could I really live with myself if I let them all die?' He had no idea what had happened to Ernie, or if he would ever see him again, but he knew he would never be able to look his friend in the eye again if he walked away now. It was hard for him to find the courage, but he knew it was absolutely the right thing to do.

Bruce straightened his tentacles, lifted his head up and pulled his shoulders back. Although he didn't really feel it, he shouted, 'I am a tough Aussie snail. I can at least try!'

Quickly, Bruce slid back through the hole in the fridge and onto the top of the box. 'Hey, snails. Up here!' he yelled, peeping through the flap.

'How did you get out there?' they yelled.

'Never mind that,' he replied. 'Let's just get you out here too.' He could feel himself beginning to stiffen with the cold again. Thinking quickly, he launched himself off the side and dived into the warm avocado. This time he made sure he emerged completely covered in the green mush. Now he had his very own green thermal jacket.

Meanwhile, the snails in the box had managed to push open the flaps of the cardboard box. Excitedly, Bruce slid over to meet them.

'Argh! Run for your life!' they yelled. 'It's a green, scary, snail-eating bug thing!'

Bruce chuckled to himself and was tempted to play along for a while, but thought better of it. 'It's me, Bruce!'

They all held their breath and looked at him, puzzled. It sounded like Bruce, but it sure didn't look anything like him.

'G'day, cobbers!' he said in his strong Aussie accent. Everyone exhaled with relief.

Now he had their attention. 'OK. I have a plan!' he announced.

Everyone cheered with excitement through chattering teeth.

'But we have a lot of work to do and we have to move quickly.' Bruce looked around. Every boggly eye was looking straight at him, every slimy jaw was wide open, and every snail was hanging on his every word. 'Right, I need you one at a time to head to those avocados down there and cover yourself in green mush, like I have. This will keep you warm as you make the long climb up to that hole at the top of the fridge.'

As he finished his sentence they all looked up and gasped. Some had never climbed that far, and they were terrified at just the thought. 'We can't, Bruce. It's too high for us. We'll never make it,' many of them shouted.

'Listen, snails, you can't give up now. You must never say you can't; you must try. There's no such thing as failure – only failure to try.' Bruce surprised himself with his own words. Maybe Ernie was finally having an effect on him. 'OK, so who's going first?'

'We will, Bruce!' shouted voices nearby, as snails began diving gleefully into the warm avocados, disappearing under the green mush and emerging in their new green jackets. Instantly they felt warmer. Then Bruce led the way to the top of the fridge.

Soon, hundreds of small, green and slimy fridge monsters were on their way to freedom. One by one they popped themselves out through the hole and found themselves in the gloomy kitchen. It wasn't long before every last snail was out and not a single space remained on the top of the white fridge. Bruce let out a sigh of relief. 'Safe at last,' he whispered, and they all smiled back at him with relief.

Just then, they heard a noise. Turning towards the door, they gasped as the same chef who had captured them walked into the kitchen and stomped over to the fridge.

The big town

The bus driver turned up the radio and began to sing loudly and tunelessly to his favourite song as the bus pulled away from the stop and headed towards the next. The bus was empty and he allowed himself unashamedly to miss every note as he wound along the roads towards the next village. Under the seats at the back of the bus, Porscha and Rose tried desperately to cover their ears as they slid from side to side with every bend in the road. The snails had sensibly slid off and were now sticking to the floor as they watched the cats slide helplessly past them, back and forth, growing dizzier and dizzier. Luckily, the driver was so distracted by the sound of his own voice that the cats went unnoticed.

Ernie looked at Porscha who was beginning to turn green and looked like she was about to throw up at any minute. Eventually, Rose managed to hook her tail around one of the seat legs and stop herself moving. As her sister flew past her once again she grabbed her paw. Quickly, the two cats jumped onto the back seat and slumped down in a heap together.

'Wow, I won't be doing that again in a hurry,' said Rose.

Porscha was still feeling too sick to even talk.

'Slide up here!' called Rose, as she peered over the seat and looked down at the two snails. They were leaning in unison with each bend, their green squidgy bodies stretched to the limit as the bus took the sharp corners. Rose couldn't help chuckling – they looked so funny.

The snails looked up to see Rose looking down at them and didn't need asking twice. Hastily, Ernie directed his grandpa up the chair leg and onto the seat. Without his glasses Manuel could only make out fuzzy shapes, and he had quite a shock when his slimy body touched the velvet seat covers. He began laughing hysterically.

Ernie looked up at him, puzzled, rolling his eyes. 'What in the world is so funny?' he asked, wishing his papa would take things a little more seriously.

'It tickles, Ern; you've got to try it,' replied Manuel as he slid across the seat.

Ernie caught up with him, and he instantly felt the short fibres tickle his soft, slimy belly. The pair laughed so much they rolled on their backs inside their shells.

The cats looked at them and laughed as the bus turned another corner and the snails rolled across the seats in their shells to join them. Suddenly Rose felt something sharp digging into her neck. As she scratched the area with her paw, something fell out and bounced on the seat.

'It's your glasses, Papa!' yelled Ernie, as he picked up the slightly bent pair of tiny spectacles which had fallen from Rose's fur.

'What a relief!' shouted Manuel, as he put them on. Suddenly the world around him became clear again.

'What now?' said Ernie as he caught his breath.

'I guess we get through this bus ride, and then the next one. Then we ask that question again,' replied Manuel.

'But what about the cats?' asked Ernie. 'They have to get back.'

'That's OK. We will,' replied Porscha, feeling brave. She was secretly enjoying the adventure of it all.

The snails were secretly relieved to have the kittens with them as it made things much easier, and a lot more fun.

Eventually, after what seemed to be a very long time, the blazing sun, which had been beaming in through the window for the whole journey, turned to shade as huge buildings blocked out the light. The winding, bumpy roads had now become straight and smooth, and the bus slowed right down as it made its way through heavy traffic. Outside the window there was a lot of noise: car horns beeping and people shouting. Ernie had only ever read about big towns in his school books, but he quickly guessed that they must be in the big town of Vélez Málaga, the first stop of their journey. 'Looks like we're here!' he shouted to the others, who had fallen asleep.

Once again the snails slid up onto the cats' backs and the group made their way along the floor, under the seats, towards the front door and waited patiently for the journey to end.

'I'm not sure about this, Ernie,' whispered Rose to the snail on her back.

'Don't worry, Rose, we just have to be brave,' said Ernie, trying to make her feel better, and hoping it would stop him feeling so scared too.

Eventually they heard the sound of the brakes releasing as the bus stopped. The cats slid forward. Anxiously, they waited for the doors to open. There was a pause as the driver gathered his stuff, and then suddenly the doors flung open and the driver quickly jumped off the bus. Without hesitating, the kittens dashed through the door and leapt onto the warm concrete floor, just as the doors slammed shut behind them, almost catching Porscha's tail in them.

'This isn't so bad,' said Porscha as she looked around her at the huge bus station that towered above her. But as they stood there, the bus driver jumped back on the bus, changed the sign on the front and drove off. As the bus left, it revealed to them a world bigger than they could ever have imagined, even in their wildest dreams. They all stood there, speechless, as they saw before them a bustling town with endless roads and houses and tall buildings, and people everywhere. Rose fainted in shock and landed heavily on the floor, nearly splatting Manuel under her.

'I thought the fiesta was bad,' said Ernie, as he blew on Rose's face, trying to bring her round.

None of them had seen such a sight before, and it was terrifying yet incredibly exciting at the same time. The snails gasped; they had had no idea there was a world so big outside of the Olive Garden and the village of Viñuela. Porscha and Manuel, however, were both feeling fearless and ready to go off and explore.

'Maybe we could do a bit of sightseeing while we wait,' said Porscha, as she looked at Manuel and winked.

'Great idea, let's go,' replied Manuel enthusiastically.

'Are you out of your mind? We've got to focus on getting to Comares,' said Ernie, 'We need to find the next bus stop and wait for our bus,' he added, feeling a renewed sense of urgency to find his friends.

Rose awoke just in time to grab hold of her sister and stop her bounding off into the town to explore. 'We can come back another time,' she said, secretly hoping Porscha would soon forget the idea.

Cautiously, the group began to wander from bus stop to bus stop, looking on each sign to find the name 'Comares'. It took a while, but eventually they found it on a large sign that towered high above their heads.

'Come on, let's go!' said Porscha, bounding off towards stop number 23.

'Wait, Porscha!' shouted Rose, who was reading the sign. 'The next bus isn't until tomorrow.'

Porscha rushed back and took a closer look at the sign.

'It says tomorrow at 11a.m.,' she said. Her head drooped down to the floor, along with Ernie's.

'I can't believe we missed it by half an hour,' he said.

'The snails might have been eaten by then,' Manuel pointed out.

'We've got to find another way!' Ernie exclaimed. 'There must be another bus.' Anxiously he began looking around him, desperate to find a way to get to Comares. 'What about a car? We could somehow jump inside one. Or a bike. There must be a bike going there.' Ernie slid down Rose's back and began heading off towards the city. Manuel slid down and followed him, having finally managed to read the sign.

'Ernie, stop! We can't do any more than we've done already,' he said.

Porscha joined him. 'He's right, Ernie. We can't just get in any car – it could be going anywhere, and if we get taken off miles in another direction there's no way we could do anything for the snails then.'

Ernie stood with his back to them and hung his head. Manuel slid alongside him, 'She's right, son. The best thing we can do is stay here and get that bus tomorrow, and hope they don't start cooking until tomorrow evening.'

Ernie knew they were right. 'OK. It looks like we'll be spending the night here, then,' he said gloomily.

'Looks like it, Ern. Come on, let's at least get some rest,' encouraged Manuel.

Gloomily, the group faced the fact that they were going to have to spend the night in this place, so they began looking around for somewhere to hide and sleep safely. Eventually they found a quiet box, tucked away under a bench, where they could hide until the morning. But Manuel and Porscha were restless, their minds racing as they thought of the world that lay just outside their cardboard box.

All Ernie could think about was his best friend.

As smug as a slug

'Get up, you quivering slugs, and fight!' yelled Captain
Pablo, as he flew at the large, slimy, green ball of slugs
that was rolling back down the wall to the compost heap,
leaving behind a thick, slimy trail as it went. 'Up! You
lazy thug slugs!' he taunted, enjoying the feeling of
power. 'You want to be like snails, you better fight like
snails and get those shells before other slugs do!'

The Boss, who had managed to pull himself to the
outside of the ball, replied, 'But they're already in the
kitchen. How can we beat them?!' They were now almost
halfway down the wall and were preparing to come face
to face with the river monster again.

'OK, I won't help you. You too lazy to have shells.
Adios!'

'OK! Please help us, your royal graciousness!' yelled the Boss through gritted teeth. 'Get us into that kitchen.'

Captain Pablo was loving every minute of this. Smugly, he danced and dived through the sky, delighting in the situation as he made them grovel for a little bit longer. 'OK, heave your butts up! Come on, you lazy slugs. You need to reverse, you stupid green things,' he yelled.

The group did everything they could to unite their strength. Soon, after a huge effort, the green ball was on its way back up the wall towards the window.

'That's it, keep going my slimy snot pile!' shouted Captain Pablo, feeling proud of his slimy recruits.

Finally the entire group reached the top. Each slug carefully manoeuvred himself onto the ledge and stood facing the window. Once again they were face to face with the fierce mob who had already conquered the kitchen, and they were now looking a whole lot angrier.

'OK, my boys! Now you move you bodies, like you strong and fit. You climb that window.' The fly buzzed and danced. 'Then, you sludgy slime, listen carefully. I tell you only once what to do. Only once, OK! You listening?'

They all nodded, without saying a word.

'Then you land on them and you squidgy them! You splat them good. OK?'

Once again the slugs nodded in obedience.

'Now GO, my feisty amigos! Rise up and charge!'

The slugs didn't need to be told twice, and together they let out a mighty 'Charge!' and slid as rapidly as they could up the glass towards the open window. They threw themselves through the opening and came hurtling down the other side, expecting a soft landing on their enemies and bracing themselves to fight. 'AARGH!' they yelled as they landed, splat, on the hard kitchen surface on the other side of the window.

The fly laughed out loud. 'Ooh, you slugs really stupid! Don't you know your own reflection?' He could hardly get his words out for laughter. 'Oh my. You funnier than those stupid snails with their stupid shells.'

The large slug tried to swat the fly.

'Oh no you don't. You need me, my hunky chunky chappie!' buzzed Captain Pablo, still laughing.

'Grrr!!' yelled the Boss as he nursed his sore head.

'What you going to do when lady comes home to find you here? Hey?'

The slugs all growled, and some began sliding back up the window.

'I tell you, she splat you flat.'

The slugs fell silent.

'Then she dry you out in sun and make insoles for shoes.'

The slugs gasped at the thought of it.

'You need me. I get you out safely. Then you take me with you to garden. OK?'

The slugs were dazed and confused, and now terrified. Left with little choice, they nodded and followed Captain

Pablo all the way up the fridge and down the other side.

It was the most glorious thing they had ever seen.
There before them lay thousands of beautiful, slightly
dusty, empty snail shells. The slugs threw themselves off
the edge of the fridge and dive-bombed onto the shells.

'Let battle begin!' shouted the fly as he watched the
slugs fight each other for the best, the biggest and the
shiniest shells. Captain Pablo just watched and laughed.

Three angry chefs

In a different village, in a different kitchen, on top of a different fridge, the snails of Viñuela watched in terror as the chef made his way into the kitchen and headed straight towards them.

'Nobody move!' whispered Bruce, although it was clear that no one was planning to move any time soon. Everyone held their breath and tried to stay as still as possible. As the man approached the cold metal box they could smell his unwashed clothes and greasy hair. Trembling, they tried to not make a sound.

Then chef opened the large white door and poked his head inside. The snails struggled to keep their composure, although some of the younger and braver ones couldn't help peering over the edge of the fridge to gawp at the bald patch on the top of his head. A few seconds later he let out a loud grunt, jumped up and hit his head on the inside of the fridge. The snails all flew up in the air with the vibration from the impact. 'Aargh!' they yelled.

'I guess he's found out we're missing,' said a large lady snail next to Bruce.

'Shh, or he'll find out we're here!' whispered Bruce in reply.

Quickly, the dazed chef pulled himself out and rubbed his sore head. Frustrated and baffled by the disappearance of his prized snail collection, along with his chance of making some money, he slammed the fridge door with all his force. Once again the snails flew up in the air. 'Aargh!' they yelled again as they struggled to keep their balance, especially the ones close to the edge.

Just as he turned to go, the chef paused for a moment, looking slightly puzzled as if he had heard something. The snails popped inside their shells, as if that would somehow make them invisible. Finally, he stormed out of the kitchen, waving his fists and yelling loudly in Spanish.

Bruce turned and looked at the crowd. In front of him, hundreds of terrified faces stared expectantly at him, waiting for an answer.

Bruce felt his heart drop to his stomach and he began to wobble in his shell. Once again he felt pressure to be the hero, and self-doubt began to cripple him. It was too much, so he turned his back on them. 'What would Ernie do?' he mumbled quietly to himself. 'Come on, think, Bruce, think!' Desperately his eyes searched the kitchen for inspiration. But nothing, not a single idea came to him. Feeling ashamed, he turned back to face the group again. But to his surprise, half of them were gone, and all that was left of them was a pile of crusty avocado mush. 'What?!' he cried, scratching his head. He pushed his way through the crowd until he came to the edge of the fridge.

There was a buzz of excitement as the snails chattered excitedly. At first Bruce had no idea what was going on, but then, out of the corner of his eye, he spotted something moving. He turned and peered over the edge.

There below him was a line of snails making their way along a cable that stretched out from the back of the fridge.

'Amazing!' he said, feeling slightly embarrassed that he hadn't thought of it himself. Eagerly, his eyes followed the cable down the wall, all the way to a plug socket on the floor below the window. There were snails all the way along it, and at the very end, standing on top of the plug were three of his teenage recruits – Franco, Paolo and Paco.

Bruce gasped and his eyes filled with tears of pride. He had trained them well. In that moment he knew that this responsibility didn't lie on just his shoulders; he was part of a team and he wasn't alone. Instantly the pressure lifted and he sprang into action to help his teammates. 'That's it, keep moving!' he called encouragingly to the rest of the snails. 'You can do it!' Some of the snails needed a little persuasion to get onto the cable, which stretched across a large distance, and it was a long drop to the floor.

Some of the younger, stronger snails were able to hook their tentacles over the cable and whizz down at a great speed, or surf down the slime from the snails who had gone before them. The strong and brave carried the small snails and those who were old and frail. Bruce was really chuffed to see such teamwork. In that moment he was proud to be a snail, and knew that they were truly a brave bunch.

Night was beginning to fall by the time every snail was safely down on the floor. They managed to take refuge under a dusty cupboard which thankfully was lit, albeit very dimly, by the light on the plug socket. The group were tired but relieved to have made it this far, and very grateful to be out of that cold metal box.

Bruce knew that they needed to come up with the next step of their escape plan very quickly. He hoped inspiration would come soon.

A close encounter

Bruce gathered his three faithful recruits around him. As he listened to the boys discussing ideas, he knew this was now a team effort and he no longer had to do it alone. With relief he let out a long sigh. The young snails were bright and their ideas inspiring. All three talked excitedly, buzzing from the adrenaline of it all. Finally Bruce managed to get their attention and put together a plan.

They agreed that they would set off at the crack of dawn, and during the night they would each take a turn on watch, just as they did in the Olive Garden. All they had to do now was to think of an escape plan, if only they knew a little more about the place they were escaping from. But they had all night to figure that out, so as they kept watch over the group they continued to discuss the next step.

It had been a long day. Soon all was quiet as every snail slipped into their shell and drifted off into a deep sleep. The boys were still chatting about the day and sharing ideas, while Bruce quietly reflected on all that had happened and thought about his friend Ernie. All seemed calm, and eventually Bruce allowed his tired eyelids to close.

'How could you lose hundreds of snails, you dimwit?!'

All the snails awoke and popped out of their shells as their eyes nearly popped out of their heads. Bruce sat bolt upright and looked at the boys. 'Stay quiet,' he breathed.

Suddenly the floor beneath them began to shake. It sounded like an elephant stampede.

'I didn't do anything; they just vanished,' came another voice.

Bruce peeped out from under the cupboard just enough to see that it was the same big man who had taken them from the garden, and this time he was not alone: with him were two others. As Bruce looked more closely he noticed that they were wearing some kind of uniform. Suddenly the penny dropped and it all made sense. 'Fair dinkum, cobbers. They're chefs!' he whispered to himself, but loud enough for the recruits to hear. 'And I know exactly what they're looking for!' he added.

'Us?' said the three recruits in unison.

Bruce silently nodded as he felt a shudder of fear across his shell.

'How could they just vanish into thin air? Maybe you left the door open, you klutz,' said the tall, skinny one. He had his head buried in the fridge, half expecting to find the snails still in there. 'Hopefully that bump will have knocked some sense into you!'

Bruce looked up at the large man as he bent down to look under the white metal box and saw a large, red, egg-shaped lump in the middle of his shiny, bald head.

'Well, it's no good blaming him,' snapped the third, who was short with a thick moustache. 'You were on guard. I guess you must have been sleeping, as usual. All you do is eat and sleep. You're good for nothing!' he added.

'Well, if you don't believe me, let's search this kitchen and find them,' said the large, bald one grumpily. 'They can't have gone far.' And the three chefs started to turn the kitchen upside down to look for the missing delicacy.

Bruce had never been so scared in all his life. He looked at his young recruits, who looked just as terrified as he felt. Then he looked around at the others. There were so many snails, young and old, and everyone was so tired and in desperate need of sleep.

'We have to do something. We can't stay here – they'll find us in no time,' whispered Paco.

'I know! I know!' replied Bruce, who was frantically trying to think, although it was virtually impossible – the chefs were making so much noise as they turned the kitchen upside down.

'I've got it!' Bruce shouted finally. 'Everyone, listen carefully! Slide up and stick on the bottom of the cupboard. It's our only chance!'

The snails didn't hesitate and they began sliding up the four legs of the dusty old wooden chopping table that they were hiding under. Bruce had never seen the snails of Viñuela move so fast. Very soon, more than half of them had made it and were safely out of sight, and the rest were still frantically on their way.

'Hey, egghead!' shouted the short chef. 'Make yourself useful and check under that chopping table.'

The snails gasped.

'Quickly!' yelled Bruce, his heart racing.

'Move, move, move!' shouted the recruits as they hauled snail after snail up from the legs to safety.

As if in slow motion, the large chef lazily dragged his feet across the kitchen floor towards them. Upside down, the snails watched as he drew nearer, holding their breath in hope that every snail would be able to get out of sight before he arrived, or they would give the game away for all of them.

Suddenly he paused. 'Which one?' he said gloomily, dreaming of his bed and yawning with tiredness.

'Miguel, how many wooden chopping tables do you see in this tiny kitchen?' yelled the tall skinny one, who had his head buried in a box of rotten vegetables.

'Er, one, I think,' he replied, after a long pause.

'Well, then, which one do you think I'm talking about, stupid?' said the short one as he twiddled his long moustache, growing more and more frustrated with his colleague.

'Oh, OK,' he mumbled, and he began to walk slowly towards the snails, dragging his feet along the wooden floor.

Finally, the recruits pulled the last snail up onto the underneath of the cupboard. 'Shh!' whispered Bruce. Everyone became completely silent, hanging upside down using every ounce of their suction slime to not fall off the dusty wooden surface.

Slowly, the chef tilted the cupboard and bent over to look underneath. He was just about to put his bald, greasy head under it when his mobile phone suddenly rang loudly, deafening the snails for a few seconds. He let go of the cupboard and it dropped back onto all four legs again.

'Whoa, hang on!' the snails shouted as it crashed down, causing some of them to lose their grip and fall to the floor. The large chef fumbled desperately to find his phone in one of his pockets, but he had so many it took him a while.

Many of the young snails, unaware of the danger of their situation, began bopping to the musical ringtone on the phone, as the chef searched his many trouser pockets. 'Will you answer that thing, Miguel?!' yelled the short one as he stood on the kitchen worktop and checked a high shelf that was filled with pots. 'I hate that song,' he added.

Finally, Miguel found the phone in his shirt pocket and answered it. 'Yeah, what?' he said abruptly, feeling flustered and stressed.

'Is that how you talk to your boss?' yelled the voice on the other end of the phone. He was shouting so loudly, the snails could hear every word.

The chef immediately changed his tone. 'Um, yes sir. I mean, no sir. Sorry, I mean, Mr Mayor,' he stumbled over his words.

'Tell me you have found those snails, you blubbering greaseballs,' said the mayor.

'N- n- not yet sir, but we will, I'm sure of it,' replied Miguel. The snails could hear the shaking in his voice.

'Well, that's not good enough. If you don't have them by first light tomorrow I will personally make sure you never work in a kitchen again. All of you!' And with that he slammed the phone down, leaving the chef trembling in his boots.

'I told you they're not in here!' he shouted at the short chef who was still on the kitchen worktop. 'Let's get out of here. We need to think of a new plan – and quickly!'

The third chef, whose head was still in the box of vegetables, stood up. 'I have an idea!' he said enthusiastically, as a mouldy courgette slid down the side of his face.

'This better not be one of your dimwit plans, Fernando,' said the short chef as he hopped down off the counter, leaving muddy bootprints along the work surface.

'Nope, it's better than those ones. We'll set up water sprays around the village so those stupid snails think it's raining and come out of hiding. Then we'll grab them.' He smiled to himself, knowing it was a good plan.

The other chefs both rolled their eyes. It wasn't exactly a new idea, but it was all they had. 'Just let me get near them and I'll gladly step on them with my big boots so their faces meet the pavement,' growled Miguel, who now had a personal vendetta against them.

The snails under the cupboard gasped; many more lost their grip and dropped to the floor.

'Listen, both of you!' shouted the short one. 'There will be no splatting. We need ALL of the snails alive!'

Then the three men picked up some large boxes and began to make their way out of the kitchen. 'Hey, Miguel, if the sprays don't work,' said Fernando, the tall skinny one, still with the courgette on his face, 'I can do a tribal rain dance.' He began making up silly chanting sounds and danced his way out the door.

When all was finally quiet, the snails who were still stuck underneath the table slid down and checked on the ones who had fallen. Thankfully no one was injured, but everyone seemed to be shaken up and exhausted – apart from the young ones who were still singing and jigging to the phone tune and getting on everyone's nerves.

With the chefs out of the way, the snails finally managed to get a few winks of sleep before dawn broke. Bruce and the boys stayed awake and tried to think of a great 'escape from the kitchen and death by paella' plan, but no matter how hard they tried, nothing seemed to come to mind, and soon they, too, fell asleep.

Poised for adventure

All was quiet at the bus stop in the middle of the city. Inside an old, dirty cardboard box under a bench, two snails awoke, just as the sun was coming up over the buildings. Nervously they poked their heads out of the box. To their relief there was no one around, and all the buses were parked up at their bus stops, waiting for their drivers and for the day to start.

Ernie slid out of the box, stretched his tentacles and yawned. 'Looks like a good day to rescue some snails,' he said, feeling more positive after a long sleep.

Manuel slid out to join him. 'It's beautiful, isn't it?!' he said, looking round at the clear blue sky and the stunning buildings towering over the bus depot.

Between the buildings and statues were beautiful large green trees. Ernie was surprised to see them and wondered if there were snails living there. 'It sure is, Papa. Let's come back here one day and explore.'

'Yeah, we'll come back with Bruce and the others.'

Ernie liked his way of thinking. 'Good plan! Come on, let's go!' Ernie called to the cats who were still sleeping.

'Typical teenagers!' said Manuel, as he rolled his eyes.

Once the cats were up they emerged cautiously from the box and together they all wandered over to the bus stop. Ernie noticed that Manuel and Porscha seemed to be dawdling. 'Quick, Papa!' he called.

'What's the rush, son? This place isn't as scary as it seems,' replied Manuel, as he meandered along the concrete floor taking in the sights of the new world around him.

Finally they found the bus they needed and hid under the front wheel by the door to wait. 'Papa, sometimes I really wonder who is the older and wiser one out of the two of us. You seem to get younger as you get older. It's not safe for us, and you know it,' chided Ernie.

Manuel rolled his eyes and smiled at Porscha: he had grown too old to be so serious.

They didn't have to wait long: soon people began to arrive. First were two cleaners who washed the floors and emptied the bins. They were followed by two waitresses who came and opened the cafe next to the bus stop. Manuel watched as a lady put chairs out, turned on the coffee machine and began to press fresh oranges. His mouth began to water as he dreamed of drinking the fresh juice. 'Can you smell that, Ern?' he said. 'It smells incredible!'

Ernie agreed but didn't say anything. Deep down he hoped that one day he would come back here with his papa and try all these wonderful things.

All seemed to be quiet outside the bus stop except for the sound of the occasional car driving past. But with every minute that passed, the noise from the town around them grew louder as it began to awake, until soon there was an orchestra of different sounds closing in on them like storm clouds.

'I hope our driver comes soon,' said Rose, feeling unsettled.

Finally, the bus drivers began to arrive for work. Patiently the cats and the snails remained hidden under the wheel as they waited for the driver of their bus. Inquisitively, Manuel and Porscha watched as the big world around them came to life, fascinated by the different things the humans did, and thinking they were not that different from snails and cats. Ernie, however, was growing more concerned about his friends by the second; he knew anything could have happened to them all by now. Rose sensed his anxiety, 'Ernie, we *will* rescue them,' she said, hoping to ease his mind.

'I know, Rose. I don't doubt that,' he said, taking encouragement from his own words.

Ernie looked across at his papa. He didn't seem concerned in the slightest, but he knew that was because Manuel had learnt to try not to worry about anything. He often reminded Ernie that worrying doesn't achieve much except to make you miserable. Ernie knew he was right, but somehow he could snap out of it.

The drivers greeted each other and grabbed coffees and sandwiches at the cafe. They seemed quite friendly, laughing together and asking about each other's families. Ernie, too, thought to himself that they were not so different from snails.

When they had finished chatting, the drivers all went off to their buses and opened the doors. Ernie and Manuel watched as a small man with thick black hair walked in their direction.

'This must be our driver,' said Manuel.

'Looks like it,' agreed the cats.

'Let's get ready then,' added Ernie.

Sure enough, the man walked to their bus and unlocked the door. The cats waited, poised and ready. The doors slammed open, hitting the side of the bus and causing it to shake a little.

'Wait!' whispered Porscha. She was at the front and could see the most, so they waited for her signal. Once the driver was settled in his seat, he pulled out a clipboard and began to fill it out.

'Now's our chance. Let's go!' she said. The snails were already on the cats' backs. Cautiously they crept up the steps of the bus, then past the driver. By now he was standing up, changing the sign on the front of the windscreen. They had a clear path. They made their way safely under the seats and began to creep quietly towards the back of the bus.

It wasn't long before people began to arrive. The bus filled up rapidly, and soon most of the seats near the front were full.

'I wonder if these people are going to the festival,' whispered Ernie.

Just as Manuel was about to reply, the doors closed with a loud bang. The bus pulled away out of the city and began its journey through the busy streets lined with enormous buildings. Once they set off, the cats jumped up onto the back seats, which were thankfully still empty, and sprawled across them. Both the cats and the snails loved the feel of the velvet seats.

The cats kept watch just in case someone decided to move to the back seats, while the snails enjoyed listening to the different conversations going on around them. Ernie was fascinated by the different things the humans talked about, like clothes and money, although he thought it all sounded very complicated. Eventually he grew bored of their chatter and looked around him. He saw a narrow rim by the window, just wide enough for a snail to sit on and look out. 'Papa, want to do a bit of sightseeing?' he asked his adventurous grandpa.

Manuel smiled. 'Sure thing, Ern. Take the lead.'

So the pair slid up to the window. It was an effort, but when they made it they realised that it had all been worth it.

For about 20 minutes the bus chugged slowly through the narrow streets and bustling traffic; then it turned a corner on to the highway. Sunlight flooded the bus, and for a second the snails were blinded. They squinted, and when their eyes had adjusted, they saw before them endless fields of fruit and vegetables. The snails gasped and squashed their squidgy noses up against the window. It was a snail's dream come true; it made their Olive Garden seem almost like a speck of dust.

Cars whizzed by as the bus gained speed, and the snails felt dizzy as they tried to focus on the sights around them. After a short while the bus slowed down and turned off the big road on to a smaller and quieter one. It then crept along slowly, swerving to avoid the potholes. Then, after no time at all, it began to climb up into the mountains on a windy ascent to the stunning village of Comares.

The view was spectacular. They could see right across the mountains, over the tops of villages which now seemed so small. Even the big town they had just left seemed like a dot on the horizon. They followed the view all the way to the sea, which stretched out as far as they could see. Ernie and Manuel were absolutely speechless. They had had no idea that the world was so big and that they were so incredible small, and they certainly had had no idea just how beautiful their world was.

'Wow, how small we must be,' said Ernie.

Manuel could only manage a nod.

The journey seemed endless, and the snails soon fell asleep with their faces stuck to the window.

Eventually the bus slowed right down and signalled to turn right. The snails awoke and peeled their faces off the glass just as the bus turned the corner. Excitedly, they spotted a beautifully decorated sign welcoming them to the small traditional village of Comares.

'Porscha! Rose! We're here!' yelled Ernie to the cats, who had fallen asleep too.

The cats woke up, looking dazed and confused.

'Up here!' he shouted.

Without hesitation they put their front paws up on the window ledge and looked out. 'Wow, it's so beautiful,' said the cats, spotting the beautiful mosaic sign.

'I want to live here,' said Manuel.

'Me too,' agreed Porscha, as the bus passed through a beautiful Moorish arch. The little group stared, in awe of it all. However, their amazement was short-lived and soon turned to terror as Ernie pointed, speechless, at a large banner that hung across the arch. It was proudly advertising 'SNAIL PAELLA'.

The banner brought them back down to earth with a bump and they fell off the window ledge in shock, landed on the seat below and bounced a few times. Finally the bus screeched to a sudden halt as it reached the bus stop near the town square, causing the snails to fly through the air and hit the back of the seat in front of them. Luckily, everyone else on the bus was too excited to notice what was going on at the back. It wasn't long before people were out of their seats and pushing their way to the front, eager to get off.

'Come on!' shouted Rose, as she watched the snails emerge dizzily from their shells. 'Get on my back; we don't have long. Everyone is almost off the bus!' Then she jumped off the seat with Rose following close behind. Ernie and Manuel barely had time to slide onto the cats' paws when Porscha daringly shot off through the people's legs and leapt off the steps onto the hot tarmac below. Rose had no choice but to follow, hoping they would go unnoticed.

'Whoa, slow down! We're not on properly!' yelled Ernie, clinging on for dear life.

'Are you trying to kill us, girls?' added Manuel.

Suddenly they heard a loud shout coming from the bus. 'CATS!' yelled one of the passengers as she saw the girls dive off the bus.

The driver, spotting them, pushed his way through the passengers, jumped off the bus and began to chase the cats. 'How dare you get on my bus, you vermin!' he shouted, waving his fists angrily.

The cats didn't hesitate. They bounded along the road at full speed in the direction of the square with the snails hanging dangerously close to the floor, eyes closed tight with terror. 'Over there!' shouted Porscha, as she spotted a large bin. Quickly they dived underneath and skidded to a halt, safely out of danger. The snails opened their eyes and the four friends let out a sigh of relief. 'Wow, that was awesome!' giggled Porscha. Rose shot her a disgusted look.

The disappearing delicacy

It seemed to the snails as though it was only a few
minutes ago that they had finally fallen asleep. Now
everyone awoke as the new day arrived, bringing
sunlight through the window, humbling the dark and
sinister kitchen. As they looked around them and
remembered where they were, many began to panic.

'Quick, there's no time to waste panicking,' shouted
Bruce. Despite their best efforts, Bruce and his team had
yet to come up with a plan. Many of the snails hadn't
slept properly and were tired, scared and hungry. Bruce
did not want to add hopelessness to the list of emotions,
so he stayed quiet and acted as though he and his recruits
knew exactly what they were doing. The only thing he
did know for sure was that he needed to get everyone out
of that kitchen – and fast. 'Right, everyone, let's get
moving!' he shouted.

'Yes, let's hit the road, cobbers!' said Paco, mimicking
Bruce's slang. Bruce looked proudly at his favourite
recruit and smiled.

Obediently, the snails of Viñuela calmed themselves
and began to slide cautiously across the kitchen floor
towards the door, with Bruce and Paco leading and the
other boys at the back watching for stragglers. The
wooden floor was shiny, making it effortless to slide

across, which was very helpful, as everyone was still exhausted from the events of the night before.

The large group had just about reached the middle of the kitchen and were in sight of the open door when suddenly there came an almighty yell from somewhere inside the building: 'NO SNAILS?! What do you mean you can't find any?' boomed the voice. 'How can you lose hundreds of snails?'

All was quiet except for a few groans and shuffling of feet. The snails froze.

'Do you know what a delicacy snails are? My snail paella was going to be the best for miles around and restore this restaurant to glory once again.' The voice had a strong Spanish accent and sounded important. It sounded as though it was coming from a room below the kitchen.

Then came the sound of a chair sliding on the floor and the man rising to his feet. 'And now you blubbering greaseheads have ruined it. Ruined it for good!' he shouted as his fist slammed down on the table, causing the snails to fly up in the air in the room above him. 'Well, now I will make sure that you are ruined too!'

'Aargh!!' shouted the snails, and they began to slide in all different directions looking for somewhere to hide other than their shells. But all around them was nothing but floor, and the nearest hiding place was at least half an hour's slide away.

'I ask you to do one thing, and you can't even do that!' yelled the voice. 'Get out of my sight!'

Every snail instantly took refuge in their shell. Bruce turned to Paco, who was next to him. 'They must be in the room below us. We've got to keep moving – they could come back any second.' Then he turned and shouted to the others, 'Move! Now! We've got to get to safety.' The others sensed the urgency in his voice and moved as fast as they could.

* * *

Ernie, Manuel and the cats were hiding under the bin outside when they heard the yell. They looked up at the building in front of them. The voice seemed to have boomed out from a window on the second floor. It was so loud it blew back Ernie's tentacles.

'Did you hear that, Papa? They've lost the snails,' he said.

'How could I *not* have heard?' replied Manuel. 'And how could they lose all the snails?' he scratched his head and wondered.

Ernie looked at him and smiled, raising his eyebrows.

'What's wrong with your eyebrows, Ernie? They've gone all funny.'

Ernie frowned, then realised that his papa must be having a senior moment; he was quite an old snail, after all, despite the fact that he didn't think he was.

'Don't you get it, Manuel?' said Rose gently. 'They haven't lost the snails. They've ESCAPED!'

'Oh yes, of course. Well spotted, and well done to Bruce. He must have got them all to safety.'

The group watched as the three chefs walked gloomily out of the restaurant, and sat themselves down at the tables outside.

'That's him!' shouted Ernie and Manuel in unison.

'That's who?' asked Rose.

'The one who stole the snails,' answered Ernie. He began trembling just at the sight of him as he pointed to Miguel, the large, bald one. Just then, he spotted the name of the restaurant and gasped as he realised it was the same as the name on the side of the van: Restaurant Carmen.

'And there are two others,' added Manuel, who also appeared to be slightly unnerved at seeing the snail thief again.

Porscha looked at the men and then turned to the snails, sensing their fear. 'Yes, but they are the same three chefs that our friends have escaped from,' she said, 'which means, Ernie, that they're obviously not that clever.' She smiled. 'We don't need to be afraid of them, or intimidated. They are three and we are four. We'll find the others and get home safely.'

Ernie smiled at Porscha. She was brave, and he was inspired by her. 'Sure thing, girls. Those chefs are no match for us, no matter how big they are,' he said as he stood tall and proud in his tiny shell.

'Phew, but they really stink, don't they?' added Manuel, as an odour of cooking fat and rotten vegetables wafted towards them. The group let out a nervous laugh.

'Right, we just need to find where our friends have escaped to,' said Ernie bravely.

They began searching the area around them with their eyes, all the while keeping their ears on the conversation that was going on between the chefs.

The three men sat with their heads in their hands. It was obvious that they were totally baffled and clueless as to how the snails had vanished. For a moment they sat in silence, contemplating their situation and considering their career options. Then suddenly, one of them broke the silence. 'Let's go back to Viñuela for one last look. Maybe those lousy snails have somehow made their way back to that stupid garden of theirs.'

Ernie and Manuel gasped and turned to each other. 'How in the world do they know about our garden?' Ernie wondered out loud.

'Who knows, my son, but one thing I've learnt on this journey is that there's a lot we don't know about this world,' answered Manuel.

'He's right,' said Porscha.

'We'll have time to figure out those things later, but right now that's not important,' added Rose.

'Yes, we have to find Bruce and the others. We're so close,' said Ernie determinedly. 'They must be in that bar somewhere.' He slid towards the entrance to the dark Spanish bar. 'You coming, Papa?' he yelled over his shell towards his grandpa. 'I could really do with your help.' But there was no reply. 'Papa?' Realising that he was talking to himself, Ernie turned around to persuade Manuel that it was time to give in and get that hearing aid that he'd needed for so long.

But there, standing where his papa had been, were two massive boggly eyes.

'Aargh!' Ernie yelled. He popped into his shell with fright and began to roll down the hill.

Porscha and Rose began giggling out loud.

'It's me, son!' said Manuel laughing, having got his own back on Ernie from the bus stop the day before. Ernie popped back out of his shell, stuck himself to the floor and looked in the direction of his papa's voice.

The boggly eyes had vanished and he saw the small head of Manuel peering around the side of an empty glass soft drink bottle.

'Wow, Papa, that bottle really makes your eyes look big,' said Ernie, who began to chuckle nervously.

'Hey, Ern. You need to come and see this,' said Manuel with excitement. 'Quick!'

Ernie felt his heart wobble. In these last few days he had been shocked, surprised, scared, bullied and terrified, not to mention stuck to a tree, and now he had no idea what to expect. By the look on his papa's face he knew it would probably be so bizarre that he would never guess.

Ernie slid over to the bottle and looked through the open end of it. 'What is it? I can't see what you're looking at,' he said. He turned to look at his papa, but Manuel's gaze was fixed straight ahead of him, his wrinkly jaw hanging low, and a little bit of green dribble was hanging from his bottom lip.

'Up there, at the window,' replied Manuel without moving.

Impatiently, Ernie scanned all over the front of the building.

He was about to give up when his papa spoke up again. 'Ernie, look at the top window, and look at the wire next to it.'

'Wow!' said Ernie, finally seeing what his papa was seeing.

The two snails sat gazing above them in amazement, with a pool of dribble collecting on the floor in front of them.

A crash landing

From their safe hiding place under the bin, Rose and Porscha were busy washing the dust from the bus floor off their fur as they listened to the conversation between the chefs. Rose was beginning to worry. She felt that they were all way out of their depth and, although she would never tell Ernie, she worried about the fact that the chefs knew the location of the Olive Garden. She suspected that perhaps they weren't as stupid as the snails believed them to be.

Porscha, on the other hand, seemed to thrive on danger, and when she had spotted something moving up at the window of the restaurant, she had leapt to her feet and bounded towards the open door of the restaurant. When all was clear, she dashed inside and straight up the stairs. Ernie and Manuel, who were still drooling and gazing up at the window, didn't even see her go. It was only when they saw Porscha up at the window that they snapped out of their daze.

'Bruce! It's me, Porscha,' she yelled as she leaned out of the window and looked along the wall. With her eyes she followed the brightly coloured bunting which was hanging from the kitchen window on the front wall of the bar, ready for the fiesta later that day. A long line of snails was leading out of the window and moving along the bunting towards the next building.

119

There was a loud gasp, and the snails turned to see a cat looking at them from the window. A few seconds later, hundreds of excited snails began chattering. 'It's Porscha!' 'Are you here to save us?'

'I hope so,' she said, feeling a little uncertain about making promises she didn't know if she could keep. 'But where's Bruce?' she asked.

'Hola, Porscha!' came a small, distant voice. At the far end of the line was Bruce leading the whole group.

'Where are you going?' she shouted, confused as to where the bunting might lead.

'We don't know,' replied a small snail near the back of the line. 'We're just getting as far away from that kitchen as we can.'

Porscha smiled with relief. She was so excited she could hardly wait to get back and tell Ernie and Manuel about their brave friends. But she was still none the wiser as to where the snails were all going.

Back on the road, the two snails sat wondering the very same thing. Rose, who was still anxiously washing, was oblivious to everything that was going on. She was mumbling to herself, 'This journey was a crazy idea. I knew I shouldn't have said yes. Why did I listen to Porscha? She's always getting me into trouble.' She was so busy talking to herself that she didn't notice that her sister had gone. Neither did she see the large hand that came down right beside her and grabbed her two snail friends.

Ernie and Manuel, who were suctioned to the floor watching Porscha, suddenly felt themselves plucked away from the ground and lifted high in the air. It was the strangest feeling they had ever experienced – and it was not pleasant. It felt as if they were about to be separated from their shells. They hid their heads in their mobile homes as their squidgy bodies dangled in the air, wriggling desperately as they tried to find something to stick to.

Finally, they felt their bodies touch something warm. Relieved, they popped out of their shells to see what was going on, and they had the shock of their life. The large, bald chef was staring right at them, his face so close they almost went cross-eyed as they tried to focus on him.

'What do we have here, then?' he boomed.

Dazed and confused, Ernie and Manuel just stared at him. Neither of them had ever been this close to a human before. They felt a mixture of intrigue and fear all rolled into one. Manuel whispered to Ernie, 'Someone really needs to teach him how to use a toothbrush,' as they tried not to breathe in the foul stench of his coffee breath.

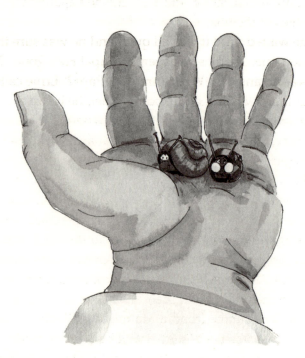

He stared at them menacingly. 'I know you've got something to do with the disappearance of the other snails. Now you're going to take me to them, or I'll separate you from your shells and eat you whole.' Then he opened the back doors of a large van. It looked like the same one that the snails of Viñuela had been taken off in.

Inside were many brown boxes, all with different labels: 'spices', 'rice', 'vegetables', and so on. The man bent down, opened the lid of a box towards the back of the van, labelled 'Snails', and threw them inside. Ernie and Manuel spun in the air and came crashing down inside the box. They managed to dive inside their shells a split second before they landed, although it didn't make the landing much easier, and they crashed against the hard edges of the box.

Ernie waited until it was all quiet and he was sure the man had gone. Then he whispered, 'Papa! He's gone.' But there was no answer. 'Where are you, Papa?' Ernie called out, but there was still no response. Then he heard a muffled groan nearby. He slid over to where the sound came from and found his grandpa. 'Papa, are you OK?'

'It's cracked, Ernie. It's not good.'

Ernie looked at Manuel's shell. He was right – his papa's shell had a large split down the side. Ernie was devastated. Most snails never survive a shell crack, and this was a big one. His shell was older and more fragile than Ernie's, and it was no surprise that Manuel's landing had caused some damage. It didn't look good for his beloved grandpa.

He slid back to the front of Manuel's shell and looked inside. 'It's not too bad, Papa. You'll be fine,' he said, knowing that it was not totally the truth. Manuel knew it too, but didn't want to show it. 'We'll find a way to fix you. Just try not to move too much.'

The two snails huddled together as the van pulled away and began the journey to Viñuela.

Snail-napped

Rose looked up from under the bin just in time to see a large chef throw something into a van and slam the doors shut. Once she realised the snails were nowhere to be seen, it didn't take her long to figure out what was going on: Ernie and Manuel had been snail-napped right under her nose. She couldn't believe that they had come this far only to watch as her friends were taken, presumably back to Viñuela, and without achieving their mission to rescue the others. Rose felt awful: if she hadn't been so busy washing she may have been able to save them.

'And where in the world is my sister?' she asked herself, realising suddenly that Porscha had gone too. Rose's heart sank; she felt very alone and far from home and could feel herself beginning to panic. Knowing that would do no good, she tried to calm herself and think what Ernie would do in this situation. 'Think good thoughts,' she mumbled to herself. But no matter how hard she tried to not think about how bad the situation was, her thoughts seemed all the more determined to wander. Desperately she tried to remember what they had been doing the last time she had seen them . 'The soft drink bottle!' she shouted, as it all came back to her.

'What were you looking at, Ernie?' she whispered as she dashed over to the bottle. She lifted it up to her eyes and quickly scanned the building through the makeshift binoculars. Suddenly she noticed that the bunting seemed to be strangely alive and moving. As she took a closer look, to her surprise she saw hundreds of snails making their way along the bunting.

'So that's where they've got to. Amazing!' she said to herself. Her eyes followed the bunting along the wall to the window. 'Porscha!' she yelled, and jumped back in surprise, dropping the bottle on the ground. Shocked, yet relieved to see her, she yelled out to attract her attention: 'Hey! Porscha, it's me!' Again and again Rose called out to her sister, but she was so far away, and the noise that was coming from the square where people were preparing for the fiesta just drowned out her voice. 'Come on, Porscha. Look at me,' she said under her breath, waving her front paws excitedly, and growing more anxious by the second.

'I hate those dirty old chefs!' came a gruff voice behind her.

Rose jumped high in the air. She looked around and found herself face to face with a ferocious-looking dog. Terrified, she leapt straight up onto the rubbish bin beside her. Unfortunately the lid was open and she fell right inside.

'I don't know why I always have that effect,' the dog mumbled to himself, 'especially on cats.' Then he hung his head, turned and began to walk away with his tail between his legs.

Rose poked her head out of the bin just in time to see him walking away gloomily. She hated dogs; they were always so unfriendly and usually wanted to chase her. But it seemed that this one wanted to talk to her. 'How strange,' she mumbled. She jumped up and sat on the edge of the bin. She looked up at her sister who was still up at the window, and then back at the dog. She felt so alone and had no idea how to rescue the snails.

'Wait!' she called, as she tried to balance on the thin edge of the bin. 'Don't you want to chase me and eat me?'

The dog continued to walk away. 'I don't chase cats,' he said glumly. 'They usually chase me, and so do all the other dogs in the village.'

She could tell from the tone of his voice that he was sad. 'What's your name?' she asked. She leapt onto the lid of the next bin, having checked first that it was closed. She was still too afraid to come down, fearing that he may be playing a cruel trick.

The dog stopped, his ears pricked up and his tail began wagging enthusiastically as he turned back to her. 'Charlie,' he said. 'I am Charlie Dog, but you can call me Charlie.'

Rose smiled. There was something quite endearing about him. He looked a little strange, with messy white hair which resembled a mop on top of his head, and his bottom jaw that seemed to stick out past his top lip. He didn't look ferocious, as she had first thought. 'I'm Rose,' she said cautiously. She jumped down from the bin and landed gracefully on all fours.

Charlie pottered over towards her and reached out his paw for her to shake. Rose, although still nervous, decided to trust him. She really needed a friend right now, and something told her that Charlie needed one too.

They talked for a little while, exchanging stories, and Rose soon discovered that Charlie's owners had left him in Comares a long time ago when they had needed to return to England urgently. Since then he had been wandering the village alone. He had managed to survive by scrounging food from the restaurant, but if the chefs caught him they would often chase him away with sticks, and he was always sad and lonely. Rose felt really sorry for him.

How could anyone be left alone like that? she wondered. She wanted to help him. But right now she needed his help. Quickly she told him her story, hardly stopping for breath. Charlie tried hard to follow what she was saying, but his brain was struggling to keep up with her, especially the bit about talking snails: he was sure it was only dogs and cats that talked. As she finished her story, she pointed up to the snails at the window.

'Wow!' said Charlie, understanding enough to know that there were snails who needed rescuing. 'That's a brave bunch of snails.' He stared at them in amazement. 'Or crazy,' he said as an afterthought.

'Yes, they are,' answered Rose. 'Brave, that is. Somehow I think they'll be OK.' She looked up at the bunting and smiled. 'But, Charlie, it's the two other snails that I'm more worried about.' Her face looked sad as she stared down the road in the direction the van had sped off. 'The chefs took them,' she said sadly as her eyes began to fill with tears.

'Oh dear, that's not good,' replied Charlie sympathetically, but unsure what to do or say next. He sat there staring down the road, his brain trying hard to catch up with the information overload. Rose wished he would say something soon, and hoped he would offer to help.

Up at the window, Porscha finally looked down to check on her sister. When she spotted the dog beside her she shouted, 'Rose, run!'

Rose looked up. 'Oh, finally!' she yelled.

'What?' asked Porscha.

'Never mind,' answered Rose.

'There's a dog, Rose!' yelled Porscha.

Rose looked at her sister and frowned. Then she looked at Charlie, the scruffy, inoffensive dog sitting next to her, who at that moment was trying to catch a fly. 'Does she really think I haven't spotted him?' she mumbled. 'Cats always spot a dog. We have a built-in dog radar,' she said to Charlie, and the pair laughed. They wondered why cats and dogs seemed to have been designed to be enemies, but neither had any idea why.

'It's a mystery of life,' giggled Charlie.

Rose looked back at her sister. 'It's OK. He's friendly.'

Porscha looked puzzled. 'Anyway, never mind that. I need to tell you something,' she called out. 'The chefs have…' At that moment, a noisy moped began spluttering its way slowly out of the square towards the main road out of the village. Before she had a chance to work out what was going on, Charlie grabbed her and pulled her up onto the back seat of the bike. Dazed, Rose looked back at her sister as the square began to move out of view. 'Viñuela!' was the only word she managed to say as the bike picked up speed and started off down the hill. She hoped her sister would figure it out.

Before Porscha even had time to think about where her sister might be going, she heard a voice from the pavement below: 'CAAAAAT!' it yelled. She had been spotted. The voice was that of a large, angry woman, and Porscha could tell she meant business.

The woman grabbed a broom and ran determinedly into the building, shouting at the top of her lungs. 'Think you can come into my bar, spreading your germs and disease? I'll make sure you never set foot in a building again!'

Not wanting to come face to face with the end of a broom, Porscha quickly moved out onto the window sill.

But there was nowhere to go from there except onto the bunting. 'Move, snails. Quick! Make room!'

The snails had no choice but to move along as Porscha hooked one of her paws over the delicate string that held the brightly coloured decorations. The snails nudged each other along, filling up the gaps between them. Porscha then put her second paw on the string, and instantly the bunting sagged under her weight.

'Whoa!' they shouted in unison. The snails feared for their lives as they wobbled dangerously on the thin string, the floor far below them. However, with Porscha hot on their trail they had no choice but to continue to move along.

'Stop!' yelled Bruce at the top of his lungs. Porscha looked over at him. He had come to the very corner of the wall. 'I can't go any further.'

All the snails stopped immediately, and stuck themselves hard onto the string as they felt themselves sliding back towards Porscha.

Just then the lady marched into the room and stuck her head out of the window. 'Where do you think you're...' She paused mid-sentence as she spotted hundreds of snails escaping along the bunting. The snails all jumped with shock: she was even scarier than the chefs.

'I think you need to come and see this, Mayor,' she said rather smugly, calling down to one of the men sitting at the table outside the bar.

'What now, Maria?' he asked glumly.

'Come and find out, my love,' she replied.

The mayor reluctantly left his hot coffee and marched upstairs, grumbling all the way.

'Aargh!' yelled Porscha. She was still almost in reach of the woman's broom. 'Move! Move!' she yelled again, forcing the snails to move along, in spite of the danger.

'This had better be good,' the mayor said angrily to his wife as he popped his head out of the window to see what she was looking at. 'I don't believe it!' he gasped. 'Snails! Hundreds of them. So that's where our paella has got to.'

By this time a crowd was beginning to gather below.

'Quick! Our dinner's getting away!' yelled the short chef, who had stayed behind while the other two went to Viñuela.

'Get them!' yelled the crowd.

The chef raced upstairs to join them. He was small and able to climb out onto the window ledge. 'Not so smart now!' he shouted in the direction of the snails as he crawled onto the ledge. But he spoke too soon, as he clumsily slipped off and landed in the dustbin below. The mayor rolled his eyes, grabbed the broom out of his wife's hands and started waving it out of the window.

'MOOOOOVE!' shouted Porscha again.

Bruce stood at the very end of the bunting at the edge of the wall. He could feel the snails behind him, pushing him forward, and although he knew he had to move, there was simply nothing for him to move on to. The pressure behind him was building rapidly. Terrified, he began to feel himself turn to jelly and he started wobbling like crazy. He was so high up, and was sure a snail could never have been this high before. As the panic behind him rose, he felt his slimy body being pushed closer to the edge – closer to his death. There was nothing he could do to escape his fate. He had no choice but to move. So he took one last look out across the mountains towards the sea, took a deep breath, and turned the corner.

Then he spotted it. It stretched out delightfully before him. 'More bunting!' he shouted with delight, as his heart skipped a beat.

Quickly he reached out and stretched himself around the corner. There was quite a wide gap but his tentacles just managed to reach the start of the next line of bunting. Quickly, he hooked them over it. He was just about to pull the rest of his body up, when the snails behind him began sliding across him. He tried to get up but they just kept coming. He could feel his body buckling under the weight as he struggled to hold on.

* * *

Whoosh! The bike pulled away at great speed. Charlie and Rose clung on for dear life. At first Rose kept her eyes closed, but when eventually she plucked up the courage to open them she was dazzled. It was breathtaking, not just because of the air hitting her fur at full speed, but also because of the dazzling view across the mountains and down to the sea.

Eventually they caught up with the van that had the snails inside. Fortunately they had just turned a corner as the moped overtook it, so they had slowed down a little. There was a small ledge at the back of the van and Rose and Charlie managed to leap off the bike and land safely on it. Then they caught their breath, sat back with relief, and watched the road snake out behind them.

A leap of faith

A gentle breeze blew around the building in the village that was high above sea level. There was a bustle of activity as people eagerly prepared for the fiesta they had been waiting for all year. They were so happy that the day had finally arrived. But it was quite a different story for a few people gathered near Restaurant Carmen, as they watched their dinner making a slimy escape.

Terrified, every snail slid forward, following the one in front as it disappeared around the corner. With no idea whether going round the corner would lead them to their death or to the next step in the journey, they had no choice but to take a leap of faith, as they were pushed forward by the threat behind them. Each one held their breath as they slid along to the end of the bunting. Many kept their eyes closed as the path took them across a slimy bridge, around the corner and on to the start of the next bunting trail. Some who were brave enough kept their eyes open; they gasped as they slid across the heroic snail who saved them from certain death.

Bruce, on the other hand, was feeling far from heroic. Somehow he had managed to turn over so his belly lay flat for the snails to slide along. It was pointless trying to get up as that would have meant that every snail who was not yet safely around the corner would still be in danger. He took comfort in that thought as his body ached in a way it never had before, and he suspected he might be stretched out of shape forever.

Finally, every last snail had made it around the corner and was safe. The only one left to cross was Porscha. As she approached the corner she noticed a very shaky, upside down Bruce, stretched out around the corner. 'Wow! Let me help you up,' she said, feeling very sorry for him, and amazed at the lengths he would go to to help others. Still hanging on to the bunting string herself, she reached around the corner, placed one paw on the other string and nestled her head gently under Bruce. 'Let go. I've got you,' she said, looking up at the frazzled-looking snail.

Bruce was so exhausted he didn't have the strength to question it. He let go of the string and allowed himself to fall through the air until eventually he landed safely on Porscha's soft fur.

'Are you OK?' she asked.

Bruce just lay there, unable to move. His tentacles were so over-stretched they hung limply down over his eyes. 'Yeah, I'll be OK,' he whimpered. He was barely able to get his words out and didn't want to make a fuss, but really he felt like an overstretched elastic band. Porscha smiled; she knew she was carrying a great hero on her head.

Once again the snails of Viñuela were spread along the bunting in their hundreds, followed by Porscha at the end. They were out of danger – for now – but no one had any idea what was coming next, and no one had seen Bruce for ages. Porscha, sensing their uncertainty and not wanting to disturb the frazzled snail resting on her head, took charge. 'Just keep moving!' she shouted loudly, so the ones at the front could hear. 'Let's get as far away from that place as possible.'

'Good plan!' shouted everyone obediently. As quickly as they could, they followed the bunting along the building. It eventually crossed to another, slightly smaller building, which seemed to be the local tourist office. Lots of people were coming in and out of it. The bunting continued past an open window. With the extra weight of Porscha, the bunting dropped down past the window frame and the snails could see inside the building. Every snail's heart pounded as they slid nervously past the busy office, hoping that no one would spot them. However, it was Porscha who faced the biggest challenge. Still suspended by only her front paws, the rest of her body hung down well past the top of the window frame. She feared that someone would surely see her.

Bravely, she followed the others and began the dangerous passing. When she was about halfway across, she heard a small, feeble voice from on top of her head: 'Wait a minute.'

Porscha paused, reluctantly, as she felt Bruce sliding down between her eyes. Cross-eyed, she looked at him, and could just make out that Bruce was looking at something inside the office.

'I've got it!' he yelled.

'What is it, Bruce?' she asked.

'Just give me a few seconds,' he mumbled.

There was a handful of people inside the office looking at maps and brochures. So far they had been too busy to notice Porscha, but she knew that could change any second. She also knew that the mayor and his wife were hot on her trail. 'Bruce, we've got to keep moving,' she said anxiously.

'Just one more second,' he answered, sliding further down onto her nose to get a closer look.

'No, Bruce. I'm going,' and with that she quickened her pace past the window.

'I've just found our ticket out of here,' Bruce shouted, with what little strength he had left.

Hastily, she continued further along the wall. 'So what's the plan, Bruce?' she asked, looking at all the snails ahead of her who were about to run out of bunting. 'We need to give them a plan.'

'I have one! And it's my best yet!' he said confidently, as he pointed to a sign in the distance that was hanging from a balcony on the edge of the square. Porscha paused to look where he was pointing. At the end of the wall was a drainpipe which led down the wall to an iron balcony which surrounded a viewing area. Beyond the balcony was a huge drop and a breathtaking view across the mountains towards the sea. 'Tell all the snails to wait for me by that sign.'

Porscha spotted the large sign that was attached to the balcony. As she read the words she gasped with shock. 'No, Bruce, it's too dangerous.'

'Can you think of a better plan right now?' countered Bruce.

Porscha, knew he was right; there was nothing else they could do, and no time to think.

'Anyway, how risky can it be? We've got snail suction slime,' added Bruce with a grin.

'Move it!' shouted Porscha suddenly.

Bruce looked behind him. A group of villagers, led by the woman with the broom, had just come around the corner and were racing towards them.

Paco and the other recruits were at the front of the group and growing anxious as they waited for instructions as to what to do next.

'Wait for me, boys. I'm right behind you!' mumbled Bruce, knowing he was too far away for them to hear.

'Look!' yelled Paco, pointing his tentacles in the direction of the villagers.

'We need to get out of here – and fast!' said Paolo urgently.

'Sure thing, amigo. Let's get this group moving,' replied Paco.

Then he slid onto the balcony rail. The smoothness of the metal rail made it easy to gain speed, and soon he was looking straight at the sign that said in bold letters 'COMARES ZIP WIRE!' The long, thin metal wire stretched out before him across the mountains.

'Geronimo!!' he shouted fearlessly, and launched himself onto it without hesitation and began to surf down it. 'Awesome!' he yelled as he gained speed.

Franco and Paolo turned to the hundreds of snails close behind them. 'Quick, follow us!' they instructed.

But many of them were not as young and as daring as the boys, and they looked terrified. Despite having already slid down a wire at the back of the fridge and along a string of bunting high up on a building, the thought of sliding down a zip wire with the ground hundreds of metres below them wasn't appealing. Sensing their nerves, Franco looked around for something that might help. 'There!' shouted Paolo, and pointed to a pile of leaves which had gathered under the sign from the tree above. Franco quickly slid down to the pile and began passing a few up to Paolo, who gave them out to those who needed them.

'This is disastrous!' cried Bruce. 'The boys were supposed to wait for me.'

Porscha was really beginning to panic. 'There's no time for that, Bruce. It's now or never!' As she looked behind her she saw that the villagers were closing in on them rapidly.

Cautiously, the snails slid one by one onto the wire. No one had any idea where it would lead, but it was better than hanging around to find out what the inside of a cooking pot looked like. Some of them used the leaf and hooked it over the wire, holding on with their tentacles to either end. Some of the brave, strong ones whizzed down, holding on with nothing more than their tentacles. And a few of the daring, younger ones, like Paco, who used to enjoy leaf surfing through the garden when it had been raining, jumped onto the wire and surfed down it as though they had done it a thousand times before.

Snail after snail bravely launched themselves down the zip wire. But the line of snails waiting on the balcony railing was long, and moving slowly.

'It's a bit like waiting in the post office,' mumbled a very elderly old snail at the back of the long line.

'Yes it is, dear,' replied his wife. 'Never mind. We'll soon be home and we can have a nice cup of tea,' she said reassuringly, secretly enjoying the adventure of it all.

Porscha, who was at the back of the group with Bruce still on her head, said, 'This is no use, Bruce, they're moving so slowly.' She looked at the group of villagers who were but seconds away from them. There was a brief pause as they both realised they knew exactly what they had to do.

'Shall we do it?' asked Porscha to the brave yet still overstretched snail sitting on her head.

'Yes, Porscha. This is the only way.'

Porscha took a deep breath. Then, after one last look at all the snails of Viñuela, she turned to face the villagers. She knew that this could be the end of things for her and Bruce, but at least it would buy the snails some time to escape.

The woman stared into her eyes menacingly. 'Well, what do we have here?' she sneered, as she was joined by the mayor. 'I don't like cats, and I especially don't like cats in my bar.' She raised the broom, ready to bring it down on Porscha's head. The other villagers watched, distracted from chasing the snails.

'Nowwww!' cried Bruce.

Seconds before the broom came crashing down, Porscha sprang over to the bunting, grabbed it with her teeth and pulled it clean off the wall. Then she turned and bounded towards the zip wire. As she passed the villagers she mumbled through the paper and string of the bunting, 'Adios, mi amiga!'

The woman stopped in her tracks, along with the mayor, and stood rooted to the spot with her mouth wide open in shock, wondering if she had really just heard the cat speak or if maybe she was going crazy.

Porscha ran as quick as she could, yelling, 'Go snails, go, go! GOOOOOO!'

The snails could barely move any faster than they already were, but still they all surged forward, sliding over one another in their hurry. Bruce held tightly to the fur on Porscha's head and smiled to himself; this was a great idea.

'Coming through!' Porscha yelled, as she leapt high in the air over the remaining snails who were still waiting for their turn. Bravely she dived off the edge of the balcony, the bunting trailing behind her. 'Grab on!' she shouted.

The snails quickly realised what she was doing, and they didn't need to be told twice. As the bunting flew past, they stuck themselves to the brightly coloured paper.

As Porscha plummeted down past the wire, the bunting fell over it. Quickly she grabbed hold of it with both paws and whizzed down the wire at great speed, with the bunting and the snails following in her wake. Any remaining snails quickly launched themselves down the wire immediately behind her.

The villagers, who had been seconds away from catching them, could only stare in amazement as their dinner escaped out of sight, along with a talking cat.

'I didn't know snails could fly,' mumbled the mayor's wife.

He tried to reply, but all that came out of his mouth was a grunt.

Flying dog

All was quiet as the van slowed down and turned into the village of Viñuela. The only evidence of the fiesta from the previous day was a scattering of debris lining the floor – paper ribbons, burst balloons, a pair of broken maracas. Rose thought that the journey had been quicker than it had been on the bus, as the van had been speeding through the narrow, windy roads, dangerously ignoring the speed restrictions.

Charlie appeared to enjoy feeling the wind blowing through his scruffy hair, causing it to look even messier. He seemed to rejoice in the freedom. Rose, however, was not nearly so excited and had been rigid with fear the whole way, her feelings a mix of concern about her friends and nerves as to the speed at which they were travelling.

When she finally saw her village, she relaxed slightly, and was relieved to finally be slowing down. Looking around her, she was glad to see that quietness had returned to her home, and equally happy that she would soon put her paws onto ground that wasn't moving.

As soon as the van stopped, Charlie jumped off and stretched out as he looked around with excitement. 'So what now?' he asked eagerly, turning to look at Rose, who was already looking for a way to get the van door open.

Thankfully the chefs were still in the front of the van, but she had no idea for how long. 'Quick! We don't have much time!' she said, ignoring Charlie's out-of-place excitement.

Sensing her concern, he jumped back up onto the ledge at the back of the van to help Rose.

'Ernie! Manuel! Are you there?' Rose called out.

Ernie and Manuel were huddled in the corner of the box, terrified. Suddenly Ernie heard his name being called. Recognising the voice, his heart skipped a beat. 'Rose? Is that you?'

'Yes, Ernie, it's me. We're here to get you out,' she said, as she stood looking at the door, which was closed tight, and wondering how in the world they were going to open it.

Suddenly, out of the corner of her eye, she saw something flying through the air. It was Charlie. As he leapt, his lips were pulled back showing his crooked teeth and making him look even stranger. Rose quickly jumped out of the way as Charlie stretched out his front paws towards the door handle. It was a beautiful sight to see, despite his scruffiness (although that really seemed to suit him): he looked so heroic and graceful. That was until he missed the door and plummeted to the floor, hitting his chin on the step of the van on the way down.

'Charlie!' yelled Rose, as she jumped down to see if he was OK.

All he could see was stars. 'Are those shooting stars?' he asked, dazed. 'Why are shooting stars out in the daytime?'

'Charlie!' shouted Rose again. 'Are you OK?'

He could hear a strange noise; it seemed to be coming from the stars. 'They're talking stars!' he exclaimed.

'CHARLIE!' yelled Rose.

Suddenly he jumped to his feet, 'What? Who? Where? Let me have 'em. I'll take 'em on. Stand back!' Finally, his head stopped spinning and he saw a strange cat looking at him. 'Rose?' he said suddenly, remembering where he was.

'Charlie, are you OK?' she asked, concerned, although suspecting that such strange behaviour was probably quite normal for Charlie.

He scanned himself for pain, but the only thing that was hurt was his pride. Embarrassed, he got up and dusted himself off. 'Well, that wasn't a good idea,' he said.

Rose couldn't help smiling to herself. Charlie was such a funny character, but so sweet and kind. She wondered if he really knew just how wonderful he was and wished that he could see himself as she saw him. 'Come on, Charlie. That was a great idea,' she said encouragingly.

'Really?' he questioned, 'If you think so. OK, let me try it again. I think I can do it this time.'

Rose, feeling quite concerned for him, and knowing the chefs could appear any second, watched Charlie jump at the door a couple more times, each time with the same result.

Worried that Charlie was losing brain cells with every bump, and unsure as to how many he had left to lose, Rose realised she would have to intervene. 'OK, let's step this up a bit,' she said. 'I'll get on your back, and as you jump, I'll launch myself off your head.'

Charlie didn't look too sure. 'Well, um…' he began, but before he had time to finish his sentence she had leapt up onto his back and was balancing there. 'Oh, OK then, looks like we're going with that idea,' he said, looking up at the small cat now sitting on his back. 'Ready, Rose?'

'As ready as I'll ever be,' she replied, feeling uncertain, but knowing she had no choice.

'One, two, three!' Charlie jumped as high as he could. When he was close to the door, Rose leapt forward, launching herself off his back. She managed to catch hold of the handle and pulled it down with force, before landing in a heap with Charlie on the floor. Both looked up as the door slowly swung open.

'Yes, we did it!' said Charlie, feeling immensely proud of their teamwork.

Just then, they heard the front door of the van open.

'Did you hear that?' they heard one of the chefs ask. From the floor, Rose could see under the van and spotted the familiar pair of dirty boots stepping out of it.

'I'll go and check the back,' replied the second chef.

'Quick, Rose!' shouted Charlie. 'In the van!' Without hesitation the pair jumped inside.

Ernie, who had been listening to what had been going on outside yelled out, 'Over here, Rose!'

Rose and Charlie followed the sound of the small voice and found an old box at the back of the van. Rose leapt over and peered inside. The two tiny snails were hard to spot in the dark, but soon she saw them nestling in the corner. 'Oh, Ernie,' she said, feeling sorry for them. Her heart sank.

'They're coming! Quick, jump in!' Charlie whispered, taking the lead.

Carefully, Charlie and Rose stepped into the large box. The snails were speechless at the sight of the dog, and even more surprised to see Rose so friendly with him.

'What do we do next?' asked Charlie. All the snails could do was stare in disbelief.

'We carry them out of here, Charlie,' Rose replied, leaving him looking slightly baffled. 'Get on my back both of you,' she continued.

'We can't, my papa is badly hurt.'

Rose looked at the elderly snail and spotted the large crack running across his shell. It didn't look good; she had to get them out of here. Thinking quickly, she said, 'Ernie, you get on my back. Charlie will take care of Manuel.'

'I will?' said Charlie, looking surprised and confused.

The snails looked back at him, terrified. They had never been this close to a dog before, and they didn't like it one bit.

'I will!' Charlie said determinedly, and leapt out of the box.

'What are you doing? The chefs are coming!' yelled Rose.

'Just give me a second.' He looked around the van. 'There must be some here somewhere,' he mumbled to himself. 'There!' he said, as he spotted a plastic black and yellow box labelled 'Toolkit'. Immediately, he rushed over to it, undid the lid and looked inside. 'Um, spanner, bolt, nope …' he mumbled as he rummaged through the contents.

'Will you hurry up, pleeeease, Charlie. They're almost here,' said Rose, getting irritated with him.

'… screwdriver, sandpaper … Here it is! SUPER GLUE!' Charlie shouted exuberantly. He grabbed it between his teeth and leapt back inside the box. 'This should fix him,' he said as he looked at the frail little snail.

Rose looked at him and melted. 'We'll have to fix him later. For now, just pick him up gently with your mouth and he can sit on your bottom lip.' Charlie looked uncertain, but he prepared to do exactly as she instructed.

Manuel quivered as he saw the strange-looking dog coming towards him. He closed his eyes with terror and braced himself to be eaten, but gently the scruffy white dog picked him up with his teeth. Manuel opened his eyes and found himself sitting on the soft lip of the dog.

By now the chef had reached the back of the van. 'What's going on here?' he yelled, when he saw the open back door. He scratched his head.

'OK, ready? Let's jump!' shouted Rose.

The dog and the cat flew out of the back of the van, taking the chef by surprise and causing him to stumble back and fall to the ground. Then Rose bounded off in the direction of the compost heap, with Charlie following behind.

Moving dinner

It was late afternoon and all was quiet as the villagers were enjoying their siesta. On the edge of the road near the park the chef lay on the floor, unconscious. After a few moments he awoke, dazed and wondering what had just happened. He was convinced that he had just been knocked down by a strange-looking dog that was holding a snail in its teeth, and a cat with a snail on its head, flying towards him. After the events of the last few days he didn't know what he was sure of any more. He shook his head, shocked and confused, and decided he must have slipped and knocked his head, which was causing him to see things.

'Get up and find those snails, you lazy lump!' The chef's thoughts were interrupted by the tall, skinny chef standing over him and bellowing at him.

As he got to his feet, he looked towards the compost heap, just in time to see the cat and dog jump over the wall and disappear. 'There's something very strange going on here,' he mumbled to himself. He was just about to tell his friend what he had seen when he spotted something moving along the wall. He turned to his friend to tell him, but he was already creeping slowly towards it to take a closer look.

The large chef joined him and the pair tiptoed over to the wall, hoping their eyes weren't playing tricks on them. As they drew nearer, a large smile began to spread right across both of their dirty, unshaven faces. 'Looks like dinner has come to us!' they said in unison, rubbing their hands together with glee. They watched in absolute amazement as hundreds of snails were making their way along the wall towards the Olive Garden.

'Miguel, quick!' whispered Fernando, the skinny and rather bossy one. 'Set a trap before we lose them again!'

'Sure thing,' replied Miguel, who was still nursing the big red lump on his head.

'How stupid do those snails think we are?' whispered the tall one called Fernando. 'Didn't they think we would catch them again?' The pair laughed smugly to themselves as they imagined the mayor's face when they returned with so many plump, juicy snails.

* * *

They didn't waste any time. Quickly, they grabbed the large net from the back of the van and placed it at the end of the wall, out of sight of the unsuspecting snails. The chefs couldn't take any risks; they had come to understand just how sneaky these snails could be. This way the snails would fall off the wall and into the net before they had time to escape. Secretly, they were both sure that there was something going on that they didn't know about, that the snails were actually rather smart and able to communicate with each other, but neither would admit it to the other as they were too proud to allow the other to think they were crazy.

'Hey, these are fatter than the others, don't you think?' said the chef called Miguel, as he licked his fat lips.

'You're imagining it, you dimwit. They're the same ones. Look, they're heading back to that lousy olive garden of theirs,' he said smugly.

'Yep, and the only olives they'll be seeing are the ones in the paella!'

Both laughed smugly as they watched each snail drop unsuspectingly into the net.

As Rose bounded onto the compost heap, she thought her heart would burst with joy as she saw her mum, Estella, waiting for her there.

'Mum!' she yelled, 'You're OK!' But as she ran forward to give her mum the biggest hug she had ever given her, Estella's back went up and she hissed at the white scruffy dog which was bounding ferociously towards her.

Estella leapt forward with all the strength she could find, ready to sink her claws into the scruffy-looking dog.

'MUM, STOP!' shouted Rose. 'Charlie is here to help!'
But it was too late; Estella was already sailing through the
air in Charlie's direction.

Charlie had just seconds to put Manuel down before
the scary cat came plummeting down and landed right on
top of him. They rolled across the compost heap, then
eventually stopped by the water's edge, both covered in
bits of food.

As a banana skin slid down the side of his head,
Charlie said, 'Hi, you must be Estella?'

Estella, jumped up and shouted, 'What do you want
with our family?!'

Charlie looked a little offended. 'Nothing. I just came
to help Rose rescue the snails.' He looked at Rose. 'We've
had a quite an adventure,' he said, smiling at his new cat
friend.

Rose giggled as the banana skin slid down his face and
hung right on the end of his nose.

'Hey, look up there!' yelled Estella, as she was
suddenly distracted by a movement in the corner of her
eye.

The group looked up to where she was pointing and
saw what looked like the top of the wall moving. They
knew straight away that it was snails.

'Oh my goodness, it's them – Bruce and the others.
How in the world did they make it all the way here?'
cried Rose.

'I have no idea, but nothing surprises me about Bruce,'
said Ernie, feeling very proud of his friend. Estella
jumped to her feet and brushed off the food that was
stuck to her. They were all about to run across to the

snails in excitement, when suddenly the two chefs appeared and began tiptoeing towards the snails with large nets in their hands.

'OH NO!' yelled Manuel.

'I don't believe it!' cried Ernie.

They watched in disbelief as every last snail slid along the wall and dropped unsuspectingly into the large net below them.

'Nooooooo! It can't be!' Ernie's heart fell to his stomach as he watched the last of the snails fall into the net. The chefs picked up the net and headed off to the van. He had failed his friend. 'We have to rescue them, Papa,' he said, and began to slide in the direction of the van.

Unable to move very much, Manuel reached out from his cracked shell and laid a tentacle on his grandson's shoulder. 'Ernie, stop. There's nothing more we can do. We've lost them.' And he slumped his head down.

Ernie looked at him in shock. 'Papa, I can't give up that easily! I'm going!' he yelled as he wriggled away from his grandpa's embrace.

'Ernie, today I have lost my whole family. I'm not about to lose you too,' Manuel said firmly. But Ernie continued to slide away from the group.

Rose lowered her head and whispered, 'He's right, Ernie. There's nothing you can do now. We've tried everything. Now we need to fix your papa.'

Ernie knew they were right. Defeated, he slumped down and disappeared into his shell. After everything they had been through, this loss was too much to bear.

Manuel felt the same way, but he was old and wise and had learnt how to deal with tragedy. He managed to hide it better, but inside he was devastated. He knew he had to be strong for his grandson.

Charlie and Rose opened the tube of superglue and stuck the heroic and wise old snail back together again.

'Come on, Ernie. Let's get back to the garden and save what's left of it,' said Manuel, trying to be positive. 'Charlie, let's show you this garden of ours.'

Charlie smiled, feeling very sad for the two snails in their time of great loss.

Paradise lost

The water was calm and peaceful as the two snails rode in silence on José's back. It was a glorious afternoon. There was not a cloud in the sky, and bright sunbeams broke through the olive trees to make dappled patterns on the riverbank. But for the snails, there may as well have been black skies and thunderstorms, as that was how they felt inside – dark and gloomy.

Bravely, Rose and Estella faced their fear of water and followed behind. Charlie was a confident swimmer but not particularly graceful. He paddled behind the cats, looking like a drowning rat.

A few minutes later the group emerged from the warm, clear river. Charlie and the cats looked to be half the size they had been before they went into the water. The cats had done well to hide their phobia of water, and they gently shook themselves dry. Charlie, on the other hand, was less subtle, and he shook himself all over with great force. The rest of the group watched, fascinated; his head spun, causing him to go cross-eyed, and his legs wobbled in all directions as he covered everyone in a spray of smelly wet dog. Normally Ernie would have laughed until his belly ached, but instead his heart sank deeper in his chest as it made him miss his good friend Bruce and the times they had laughed together.

Dragging their tentacles along the leafy floor, the snails led their friends into the garden they had once called paradise. Now, though, it felt like the worst place in the world as it only served as a reminder of what they had lost. Gloomily, Ernie took them over to Lemon Harbour. The cats and Charlie followed respectfully, in silence. Charlie stared at the trashed cafe and imagined it full of snails, alive with laughter and chattering. Manuel sat on the bank in silence. Eventually Ernie and the others joined him, and they all sat staring at the garden, overwhelmed with sadness.

'Woooohooooo!' came a voice from up in the trees.

The cats jumped up and raised their backs, hissing at the empty trees over their heads.

Charlie made a funny attempt to bark, which sounded more like a frog with a sore throat.

'Did you hear that, Ernie?' said Rose.

'Hear what?' replied Ernie, who could barely hear anything from where he was buried, deep inside his shell.

'Coming through!' came the voice again.

'There it is again,' said Charlie, as he began barking again in his strange, gruff bark.

'Ernie, grab a leaf, roll it up and listen,' said Rose firmly.

Reluctantly, Ernie did as he was told. 'I don't know what you're on about,' he said. 'It's probably just noises from the village.' Then he put the leaf to his ear and listened. 'Whoa!' he yelled with excitement. 'Papa, did you hear that?' Ernie handed the leaf to Manuel.

'Hear what?' asked Manuel, unenthusiastically.

'Just listen, Papa.'

Manuel, who was a little hard of hearing even with the leaf, was quite sure he could hear voices from up in the trees. 'I recognise that voice,' he said, with growing excitement.

Ernie quickly rolled up another leaf and listened too.

'Wooooooooo!' came another voice.

'Yes, yes, Ernie, there's definitely someone up there.'

They all remained quiet as they listened to what sounded like hundreds of excited voices coming from somewhere above them. Eyes darted everywhere as they looked around, anxious to see where the noise was coming from.

'Wow, this is awesome, Bruce!' came a small excited voice.

'Geronimo!' came another.

'Ernie, it's Bruce and the others!' shouted Manuel. 'But that's not possible,' he added.

'I know, Papa. I heard it too. It's a miracle,' replied Ernie, still baffled as to where the voices were coming from.

Then they heard a familiar voice coming from above their heads. 'Out of the way!' it yelled.

They slid in all directions, unsure as to where 'out of the way' would be. Just then, Bruce came hurtling through the air attached to what looked like a thin wire, and made a crash landing on the soft leaves in front of Ernie and Manuel.

'G'day, cobbers!' he said breathlessly. 'It's a ripper of a day for flying.'

Ernie and Manuel tried to speak, but nothing but air came out; their small snail brains were whirling in overdrive.

Bruce began to shake off the leaves and mud which had stuck to his slimy body. 'Have you been here all the time?'

Ernie couldn't answer.

'Wow, you missed out on one awesome humdinger of an adventure, mate.' All Ernie could do was stand in shock.

'Watch out!' shouted Bruce suddenly, and he dived forward and pulled Ernie out of the way.

'Incoming snail!' shouted the next snail as it arrived in the garden.

'Incoming fly!' echoed a voice behind him. It was Captain Pablo, who came buzzing into the garden.

Finally finding his voice when he noticed the annoying fly, who he was sure he had seen the last of some time ago, Ernie questioned, 'What are you doing here?' He turned to his friend, 'Bruce, what's he doing here?'

Before Bruce could answer, whoosh, another snail came hurtling through the trees on a wire, landed under a pile of leaves and bumped into Bruce, causing him to fall forward.

'He's not with me!' mumbled Bruce with a mouthful of leaves, but before he had time to pick himself up, another snail came down the same wire.

'Ooh, here come another slimy one, moving very fast,' buzzed Captain Pablo.

Very soon, snails began to whoosh down through the trees from all directions.

'And here number 27. He young. He fast. He taking lead,' buzzed Captain Pablo. 'Nooo, but wait. We have small wrinkly one overtaking. Can he do it? Yes, I think he can,' the fly shouted as Ernie tried to block him out. 'Ooh, nicely overtaken,' he buzzed, doing a little dance in the sky.

'Just in time for tea,' said the elderly snail's wife, who was already on the ground and cheering her husband on.

One by one the snails arrived, each one making a grand entrance into the Olive Garden.

Ernie looked at his friend. 'Bruce, you can explain later, but let's get these snails out of the way, otherwise it will soon be dangerous.'

Bruce turned to him. 'Sure thing, cobber.'

Ernie burst out laughing. He had missed his friend's funny way with words.

'What's so funny, Ern?' asked Bruce.

'I've just really missed you, my friend.'

Bruce smiled. 'No time to waste on mushy stuff. We've got snails to save, Ern.'

'OK, who we have next? He is hefty. He is chunky. Ooooh, can he make it? I don't think so!' buzzed Captain Pablo mockingly, unaware of Charlie jumping up and down and wagging his tail in excitement next to him. Suddenly Charlie's tail whacked him and swatted him straight out of the garden.

'Noooooo!' buzzed the disorientated fly as his prized hat flew off his head and landed, splat, on a rotten banana on the compost heap.

'Well done, Charlie. I can't stand that annoying fly,' said Ernie with relief.

Charlie looked at him, puzzled. He had no idea what Ernie was talking about.

The two friends began to bring everyone up onto the mound and out of the way. Then Bruce went back down and guided every snail to a safe landing in the garden. Estella, Rose and Charlie then gently collected up the snails and carried them up onto the mound, where Ernie and Manuel checked them for injuries and gave them food, water and leaf blankets.

Manuel watched proudly as his grandson embraced the best of his friendship with Bruce and allowed all the other stuff that had wound him up so much to fall away. None of that was important any more. Over his many years, Manuel had learnt to drop his expectations of what he wanted others to be and to do. Instead he had learnt to love them as they were, to embrace the things about them that made them different to him and the things he liked about them, and to forget about the things that bugged him. He smiled as he guessed that Ernie had now learnt the same life lesson; it was wonderful to see.

Ernie was amazed at the speed at which the snails came through the trees. He couldn't help noticing that each of them seemed to be enjoying the experience and didn't seem afraid. When all the snails of Viñuela were safely back in the garden and had been taken care of, he slid over to Bruce. 'Somehow I don't think this is the first time these snails have done this, is it, Bruce?' he said.

Bruce laughed. 'Oh, have I got a good story for you, Ern,' he said, chuckling to himself. 'But first we have one more arrival.'

Ernie looked baffled as he looked up to the trees, his eyes scanning them for one last snail.

'Porscha, it's safe to come down!'

On Bruce's command, the cat flew down into the garden with the bunting as her parachute, leaves and branches flying everywhere. Ernie, Manuel and the two cats gasped when they saw her. Instantly, Rose and Estella raced over and embraced her.

'And have I got a story for you, Bruce!' said Ernie.

'What?' replied Bruce in surprise. 'Weren't you stuck here the whole time with Manuel? I know you were left behind.'

'Oh, are you in for a surprise, my friend. But you first, Bruce, don't make me wait any longer.' Ernie was almost jumping out of his shell to hear about his friend's adventure.

'No, no, my friend, you go first. I'm saving my story until last.'

The two looked up at the mound. Everyone was settled and comfortable, so the snails sat among the leaves and shared their stories as they watched the sun set behind the horizon, just like they had that very first time when they met on the compost heap many months ago. Ernie told Bruce how they had made it all the way to Comares by bus and were just about to rescue the snails when they were snail-napped and brought back to Viñuela, where Rose and Charlie helped them escape.

Bruce couldn't believe that Ernie had ridden on a bus. He made him tell him again in case he had heard wrong. Bruce had been so excited to tell Ernie about their daring escape out of the window and along the bunting, and he was shocked to discover that Ernie already knew. Bruce was completely overwhelmed by Ernie's story.

'But Bruce, where did you go after that?' asked Ernie, as Bruce told his story, hanging on his friend's every word.

'You'll never guess,' teased Bruce. He could see thoughts racing through Ernie's mind as he tried to guess; he was enjoying keeping him in suspense for a while.

Eventually, Bruce couldn't make him wait any longer and told him all about the zip wire.

'Oh my goodness, Bruce, that's a rip porker of a hum-dongling story!'

Bruce looked at him with a serious, puzzled expression, and then he burst out laughing. 'Ern, I really think you should leave the Aussie slang to me next time!' And the pair rolled on the floor in hysterics until their bellies ached.

By now, Manuel, the cats, Charlie and some of the other snails had gathered around Bruce and were listening eagerly to hear what happened next.

'But how in the world did you get down the wire?' asked Rose.

Porscha smiled quietly to herself as she allowed the mystery to unfold. She kept quiet, not wanting to spoil the story.

'It was brave Paco who came up with a way of us getting down safely,' said Bruce, smiling as he looked proudly at his young recruits who were busy clearing some land. 'It was super smart thinking, and to be honest I'm not sure what I would have done without him.' He looked over at Paco and the boys and smiled proudly.

'He told us all to grab a leaf and to throw it over the wire, then to hold on to each side of the leaf,' said a large snail who was standing next to Bruce, as he demonstrated with a leaf above his head.

'That's right,' continued Bruce.

'Then we all flew down that zip wire faster than you could say "Granny's apples",' said the elderly snail, who was now enjoying a cup of hot tea on what was left of his porch.

Ernie was amazed by it all, but there was one thing that still didn't add up: how in the world had they arrived in the garden?

'Paco went first. He had a huge shock when he didn't stop at the end but flew off the wire and sailed through the air,' said Franco, who had come over to join them and took up the story. He was so excited he could hardly contain himself.

Everyone gasped.

'But luckily he landed in the trees above the Olive Garden, with all the others following close behind him,' said Bruce. He paused and signalled for Paco to come over and join them.

'Bruce, this is awesome!' said Ernie, loving every second of the story.

'You bet, Ern!' He decided he would wait until later to break the news to him about the two snails from the box that didn't make it.

'Wow, that really is some story. I can't wait to meet Paco,' said Rose.

'You did well, training those boys,' added Ernie, smiling at his friend, and knowing that he had been wrong to not support him when Bruce had told him he was training them.

'Thanks, Ernie,' said Bruce.

'Hey, that still doesn't explain how you made it into the garden,' Rose pointed out.

Bruce paused and smiled. He had been wondering when someone would ask. 'Silkworms!' he said.

'What worms?' asked Ernie.

'Silkworms. They're amazing green worms that spin a beautiful yet strong yarn. They're so cool!'

Everyone's head was spinning at the enormity of the story.

Just then, a small snail slid over to join Bruce. 'This must be Paco,' said Ernie.

'Yep the one and only.' Bruce smiled as he patted Paco on his shell.

'I waited for Bruce to arrive in the trees, then using the idea from the zip wire, we managed to persuade those cute worms to spin some extra strong thread for us to create our very own zip wire to the garden. It was totally awesome!' said Paco, and then he turned and slid off with his friends.

'Where are they off to?' asked Manuel.

'You'll find out soon enough,' said Bruce, winking at Franco, who was sliding off to join Paolo and Paco, who looked to be busy creating something.

The group had listened to Bruce's story with eyes wide in amazement. They sat for a while in silence, pondering what they had heard.

After a while, Charlie broke the silence. 'Well, if you guys are all here, then who in the world are those snails who have just been captured by the chefs?'

A squirmy mass of squidgy sliminess

A beaming smile was fixed on the chefs' faces as they
drove the long, winding journey in the afternoon sun
back to Comares. They were chuffed with themselves and
couldn't wait to smugly show the mayor their huge find.
They could almost taste the steaming hot paella, and
could imagine the faces of the crowd at the town fiesta as
they tucked into the traditional dish at the summer
festival that evening. Better still, they were certain that
their dish would ensure that crowds would be flocking to
the grand reopening of their restaurant tomorrow night,
and they were sure that their boss would be so pleased,
he would give them a pay rise for all their good work.
They were so excited they could hardly wait.

The brown boxes in the back slid from side to side as
the van turned the sharp corners dangerously quickly.
The contents inside squirmed and squelched.

Finally, the van skidded into the village and came to a
sharp halt, almost taking out an elderly couple who were
crossing the road at snail's pace.

The chefs could see the mayor standing over a giant
paella dish, which was at least as big as a large dining
table. Sweat was pouring from his brow as the crowd
began to grow and press in around the famous Spanish
rice dish, plates in their hands, impatient to be fed.

The chefs flew out of the van and ran around to the back doors, opened them and then grabbed a large brown box labelled 'Snails of Viñuela'.

The men ran towards their boss as fast as they could, pushing out of the way a bunch of ladies who were busy chatting and cooling themselves with Spanish fans. The large chef then slammed the box down on the floor in front of the large pan, which was only ever brought out at fiesta time. Inside the box, the snails flew up in the air, bashing themselves against the top of the hard cardboard.

All three chefs threw on their white aprons and hats and smiled smugly at the queue that was growing before their eyes. 'You will soon be sampling the best snail paella you have ever had. I hope you're hungry?' said Fernando, the tall skinny one, as he began handing out flyers to advertise their restaurant. The short one scurried over to chat to the mayor about plans for development of the restaurant.

Meanwhile Miguel, the large one, began emptying the rice water into the pan along with spices, seasoning and mixed seafood. Once it was simmering nicely he bent down, revealing his bump which was still throbbing on his head, and opened the lid of the brown cardboard box. He chuckled to himself as he looked at the helpless snails squirming around, desperate to find a way out. 'Think you can escape Restaurant Carmen? Well, you're not as smart as you think you are, my slimy amigos!' He laughed out loud. 'Soon you will be in my belly,' he said, as he prodded his large, wobbly gut. With that he lifted the box, threw its contents into the dish and turned up the gas.

Excitedly, the crowd drew in closer, their mouths beginning to water at the thought of tasting the local speciality. As it began to simmer, the short chef took the opportunity to announce the grand reopening of the restaurant the following Saturday. The excitement continued to build as the large chef stirred the mixture with a giant wooden spoon, and the snails began to whirl around in the mixture as things began to heat up.

Suddenly, out of nowhere, a large woman, dressed in a traditional flamenco dress and holding a plate ready to enjoy some of the paella, let out a loud unnerving scream.

The crowd turned to look at the woman. Trembling, she pointed a chubby finger in the direction of the pan. She could hardly get the words out. 'It's a… a… s… s… sluuugggg!' she yelled at the top of her voice.

Everyone gasped and drew closer to the paella to take a look. Sure enough, hundreds of slimy green slugs were slithering out from the shells. 'Argh!!' yelled the ladies, as they threw their plates down on the floor and fled the park. They were disgusted, and wondered if all this time they had been tricked into eating slugs rather than snails. The rest of the crowd closed in around the pot to take a closer look. Hesitantly, the chefs peered into their precious pot and, to their surprise, they saw that the whole paella was alive and moving, a squirming mass of rice, seafood and green, squidgy slugs. They couldn't believe it was true.

The slugs were terrified. As the heat inside the pan intensified, they began to swell up in their new shells. Desperately, they ditched their useless shells and slid into the mixture, heading for the edge of the pot; they had never moved so fast in all their lives. It was hard work as they pushed their way through mounds of rice and wrestled with giant clams, which seemed to be alive and trying to gobble them inside their shells. They passed large king prawns with massive tentacles which they seemed to get tangled up in. The edge seemed so far away, and they were sure they would begin to fry before they reached it.

'Think you can cheat me?' came a booming voice from above their heads. The Boss slug paused and looked up anxiously. There, towering over the paella, one of the chefs was holding a large jar of salt. 'Going somewhere?' he asked as he laughed menacingly and began to pour the white powder into the pot. There is only one thing that slugs hate more than snails: SALT. Just the word causes slugs to tremble with fear, and just a few flakes sprinkled on one of their slimy bodies makes even the toughest slug shrivel up to a black crust in an instant.

'Get out, boys!' shouted the Boss slug.

'We're doomed!' shouted another, as he flung himself down into the depths of the paella, surrendering any chance of escape.

'Slide for your life!' yelled another as he heaved his large body across the obstacles, the heat slowing him down.

'Shh!' shouted the mayor as he put his ear down to the pot. The crowd looked at him, puzzled. He was sure he could hear something inside the pan.

'Run!' screamed one voice.

'We're barbecued dogs' meat!' shouted another.

The mayor then stood up, looking baffled, 'Talking cats, and now talking slugs. I must be losing my mind,' he said as he fainted and landed – splat! – with his face in the paella. The crowd looked at each other, puzzled, and then turned to the chefs, who were now looking very worried. Then, angrily, the crowd charged towards them with fists raised high in the air. They chased them around the giant paella pan and ran them right out of town.

Not easily broken

It was dusk. The sun had almost vanished from the horizon when the snails in the Olive Garden heard a loud scream from far off in the distance. It came from the direction of Comares and echoed across the mountains. Bruce and Ernie, who were savouring the last moments of the most spectacular sunset they had seen in ages, smiled and said together, 'I guess they don't like slug paella.' Then they burst out laughing. For a while they just sat in silence, basking in the moment and reflecting on all that they had nearly lost and had endured trying to save it.

Ernie broke the silence. 'Bruce, I'm really sorry for not listening to you.'

Bruce hung his head. He did feel sad that Ernie hadn't listened to him. He knew that if he had, maybe together they could have made a plan to protect the Olive Garden and perhaps prevented all of this from happening.

Ernie sensed his sadness and guessed that maybe Bruce needed to talk first before he accepted his apology and they put it behind them for good. 'Come on, Bruce, let it out. I'm ready to hear it,' he said, unable to look at his friend.

'Mate, I just want to tell you that if we're a team, then we have to be a team. We can't just decide one day we won't work together and the next we will,' said Bruce.

Ernie hung his head. He knew what Bruce meant. He had turned his back on Bruce and chosen not to listen to his concerns or to find out if there might be any truth in his suspicions. Instead he had been quick to just dismiss him. 'I should have listened to you, Bruce. I see that now,' he mumbled sadly.

'Yeah, Ern, then together we could have explored whether I was right or if I was just rambling. But you chose not to trust me.'

The words hurt deeply as Bruce spoke them, but Ernie knew he had chosen to not trust his friend. He didn't know why. He took some time to think about it and realised that he hadn't been seeing just how much Bruce had stepped up and changed since their journey from the compost heap, and how he had transformed from being someone who was fearful and reluctant to a great adventurer with good intuition. Ernie told him this, and that he was sorry for not believing in him enough.

Bruce sat quietly, and after a while he said, 'It's alright, Ern. I could have talked to you more and maybe that would have helped.' Ernie turned and looked at his friend as Bruce continued, 'Ern, I just expected you to believe in me and see how much I'd changed. I should have sat down and talked to you clearly about my ideas and plans.' Bruce let out a long sigh. 'I promise I will talk with you more, my friend.'

Ernie smiled. He liked the sound of that; he enjoyed conversation – he needed it. 'And I promise I will take you more seriously, my Aussie friend.'

Bruce smiled. 'Sounds like a good plan.'

The two friends laughed. They were glad to get the serious stuff out of the way so they could get on with having some fun. They knew they could have more fun now they understood each other better.

'Hey, let's have a party, Bruce!' cried Ernie so loudly that Bruce's ears were left ringing.

'What a totally awesome idea, mate. Let's do it!'

The friends quickly slid over to the boys to tell them about their idea. They found the young recruits still in the middle of the garden among the leaves.

'Hey, Paco, wanna shake this garden up a bit?'

Paco looked at him and grinned. He knew exactly what Bruce meant. 'Sure thing. That's just what we need.'

Ernie laughed and slid off excitedly to tell Manuel the plan.

He found his papa busy helping some of the families clear the debris from their broken houses. Ernie looked around. So many houses had been badly damaged; some had been knocked flat and destroyed. It was heartbreaking, as each house had been built with such love and appreciation for their new paradise home. Each had been individually decorated and was full of personal possessions. For many of the snails this was the first time they had ever had their own home, and each cherished it as if it were a part of them.

There were, however, a few houses still standing, and their owners had invited those who were homeless to come and stay with them as they all worked together to rebuild the broken houses. Ernie slid over to a small two-storey house built of mud, twigs and leaves and looked inside. Eagerly he looked for his papa, and amid the bustle of productivity he noticed the wonderful atmosphere which filled the house. With delight he watched as all the snails seemed to come alive at the opportunity to help each other, and despite the sadness at what they had lost, they seemed to have shaken it off and were getting on with rebuilding their lives. It was such a joy to see.

Ernie had felt so angry with the slugs for destroying everything he had built, for shattering his life's dreams. He hated them. He knew his heart had grown a little harder because of the hurt he felt, and although he didn't want to admit it, deep down he had believed they had won because they had taken so much from everyone. Yet now, when he looked around him and saw that people were better than they were before, even happier than they had ever been, Ernie realised that what had been intended to destroy their garden had actually brought everyone closer together – not just as a family, but as a team.

In that moment Ernie was proud to be a snail, and all the sadness that had been sitting on his shoulders fell away. He knew that the Olive Garden was not his prize that he had dreamed about for years; it was just somewhere to hold his real prize. His treasure was the strong, brave and resilient snails who were living in it. In that moment he knew that he had let go of the garden once and for all and had found something so much greater, and he no longer wanted to neglect those he loved for a stupid garden.

He smiled and almost didn't want to interrupt the work that was going on, but he couldn't hold in his excitement any more. 'Snail friends! Who wants to celebrate our victory with me?'

Surprised, all the snails stopped and looked towards the door. There was Ernie's cheeky face poking around it. 'Great idea, Ernie!' said a small, dainty, lady snail who had been busy making up extra beds.

'We have much to celebrate!' added her husband, as he arrived from the back garden with a box of vegetable scraps.

'Can we have fireworks?' shouted a small snail as he emerged from under the table and jumped up and down excitedly.

'Absolutely!' replied Ernie, although he had no idea how to make fireworks. 'We'll have the best party ever!'

Ernie looked around and wondered where the cats and Charlie were. The last time he had seen them, the four of them were sitting on the edge of the garden, chatting and laughing together. He saw that they were heading back to the river and waved to them. 'We're having a party!' he shouted, hoping they would hear him.

Charlie, who could hear even the sound of a flea jumping, pricked his ears up. 'OK, Ernie!' he answered. 'We'll be back in time for the party.' Then the four headed off towards the river and to the compost heap. Ernie had noticed that Charlie looked a little lost; he was the only one who had no home to go to.

Can snails really fly?

It had been three days since all the snails had arrived safely back in the garden. Everyone had worked hard to restore things to the way they were, and some had taken the opportunity to make things even better. There had been much preparation for the party – they wanted it to be the best party the garden had ever seen.

That night, fireworks exploded in the sky over the small paradise garden that was hidden under lemon trees and cut off by a river either side of it, on the edge of a small village in southern Spain. Music filled the garden as hundreds of snails danced without a care in the world among the rubble of their destroyed houses, as if nothing had ever happened. Every single snail was happier than they had ever been before because they knew that what they had was more than mud, sticks and leaves. It was something that could never be taken from them.

The cats arrived just in time for the food. 'Perfect timing,' said Ernie as he smiled at them.

'I never miss a party,' said Porscha.

'Yep, we know,' replied Rose, as she winked at Ernie, knowing her adventurous sister had been to many parties before.

'Hey, but where's Charlie?' asked Ernie.

'Yeah, where is that cute fella?' echoed Bruce. 'I have to say, that little pooch has almost changed my mind about dogs.'

'Come, we'll show you,' said the girls.

'What, now? We'll miss all the food,' said Bruce, who had never missed a barbecue in his life.

'We'll be back before you know it.'

The snails jumped on the kittens' backs once again. Leaving Estella to enjoy the fireworks, they quickly bounded to the edge of the garden and pointed up at a small house that overlooked the compost heap.

'I'm not sure what I'm looking at,' said Bruce.

'There, on the balcony,' replied Porscha.

Bruce and Ernie looked at the small balcony. The light from the house flooded out on to it, and there they saw a young lady sitting on a swinging chair, drinking tea. On her lap lay a very contented, white, fluffy dog.

'Oh, that's so good to see,' beamed Ernie.

'He looks super happy,' agreed Bruce.

'Yep. Well, I guess some of us don't mind being a pet,' answered Rose. She smiled, secretly looking forward to getting back to her home and curling up on the end of her owner's bed. It made her feel happy to see Charlie in a new home, and to know that he was loved.

'I hope he pops back to see us soon,' said Ernie, already missing the strange new friend he had made.

'Oh, he will,' said Rose. 'He's decided to be our very own guard dog, and to keep a lookout for any unwanted visitors to the garden.'

Bruce sighed. 'That's awesome. What a cool dude he is!' Bruce was relieved to know he wouldn't have to spend all of his time protecting the garden from now on. He could finally start to enjoy life a bit more. 'Anyway, let's head back to the party. The boys want to unveil the project they've been working on for the last two days,' said Bruce.

'Yep, and I hear it's going to be amazing!' added Ernie.

The snails slid back onto the cats' backs and they quickly went back to join the others.

The two friends slid off the cats' backs in the middle of the garden. 'Listen up!' yelled Bruce as he tapped loudly on his shell. 'We have a surprise for you!'

Everyone stopped what they were doing and the band put their instruments down. All eyes turned to Bruce.

'On our recent adventure I came to realise that many of you quite like living on the edge a little – and we're pretty good at it!' he laughed. 'I also discovered that, strangely, snails can actually fly. Who would have thought it?!' Everyone gasped and began chatting.

'Listen, everyone!' shouted Ernie. 'So for all of you who want to carry on flying, this is for you.'

At those words the three recruits came flying through the trees at great speed, somersaulted through the air and landed skilfully next to Bruce in the middle of the garden.

'We have created our very own treetop adventure,' said Bruce, as he pointed up to the lemon trees above their heads.

All eyes looked up to where he was pointing. Ernie and Bruce lit a large beacon and the whole of the treetop canopy was lit up, revealing every kind of high adventure they could think of. It even included their very own zip wire, stretching from the highest tree straight across the garden over to the compost heap.

'Wow!' said Porscha, who could hardly contain her excitement. She longed to try it, but suspected she would just have to watch the small snails enjoy themselves without her.

Sensing her thoughts, Paco called over to her. 'Hey, Porscha. It's your turn!'

She looked at him, puzzled. 'What?' she asked.

'We made it strong enough for cats, too.'

Porscha burst out laughing and bounded up into the trees and on to the zip wire. It was exhilarating as she whizzed past thousands of snails all waiting their turn to be pulled up into the trees by a brilliant pulley system which carried them in a scooped-out avocado shell to the highest point.

'Those boys are genius,' said Bruce proudly.

'Takes one to know one,' said Ernie, equally proud of his best friend for helping to bring out the genius in them.

Bruce turned to his friend. 'You ready for a turn?' he asked.

'Are you kidding? You know I can't resist an adventure.'

And the pair slid into the avocado pod and chuckled all the way up into the tree as they headed straight for the huge zip wire.

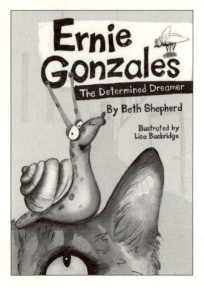

If you enjoyed this book and would like to read more about Ernie, then be sure to read *Ernie Gonzales: The Determined Dreamer*, the first book in the series. Find out how Ernie reaches his dreams, and how he meets Bruce the awesome adventurer on the way. This book is sure to bring out the determined dreamer in any reader!

If you want to be a determined dreamer just like Ernie then check out; *Dreaming with Ernie*, a curriculum-based literacy workbook to accompany *The Determined Dreamer*. Perfect for use at home or in a classroom environment. A Teacher's Guide is also available. Written by primary school teacher and literacy coordinator, Diana Mendonça.

Go to: www.erniegonzales.co.uk

For more information and to find out about more books
by Beth, go to:
www.bethshepherd.com

Look out for more books from Beth coming soon!!

Check out the amazing work by the illustrator and see
what she is working on next: www.anaitsart.com

First published in Great Britain in 2016

Instant Apostle
The Barn
1 Watford House Lane
Watford
Herts
WD17 1BJ

British Library Cataloguing-in-Publication Data

A catalogue record for this book is available from the British Library

This book and all other Instant Apostle books are available from
Instant Apostle:

Website: www.instantapostle.com
E-mail: info@instantapostle.com

ISBN 978-1-909728-51-6

Printed in Great Britain